After Hours PRESENTS
MYSTIC NIGHTS

GOOD AT IT

Denise WARNER

GOOD AT IT

LOOKING FOR A PUBLISHING HOME?

Mystic Nights is currently accepting submissions for new and experienced authors for the following genres: **Contemporary Urban, African American Romance, Romance, Silver Fox, Young Adult, Paranormal, LGBT, and Street Literature.**

Please send the first three chapters of your manuscript along with your contact information and synopsis to: <u>mysticnightspub@gmail.com</u>

We're not just a company. We're family and tutors. Come home and learn the ins and outs of the business, sharpen your skills as you go, and enjoy the opportunity to have your works professionally published in a stress-free, interactive environment.

GOOD AT IT

Recently Released from

Mystic Urban

Mystic LGBT

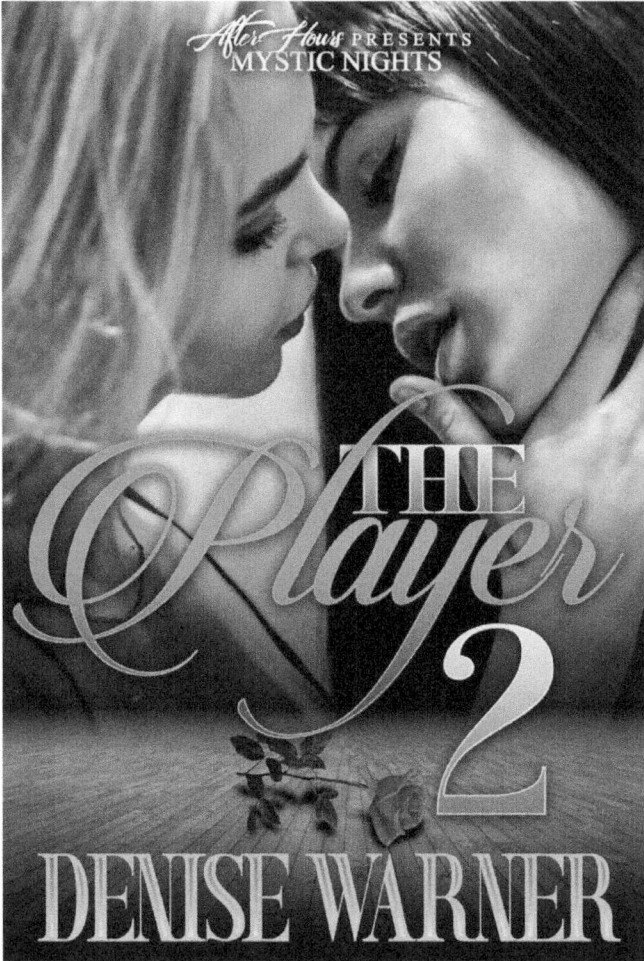

GOOD AT IT

Mystic Romance

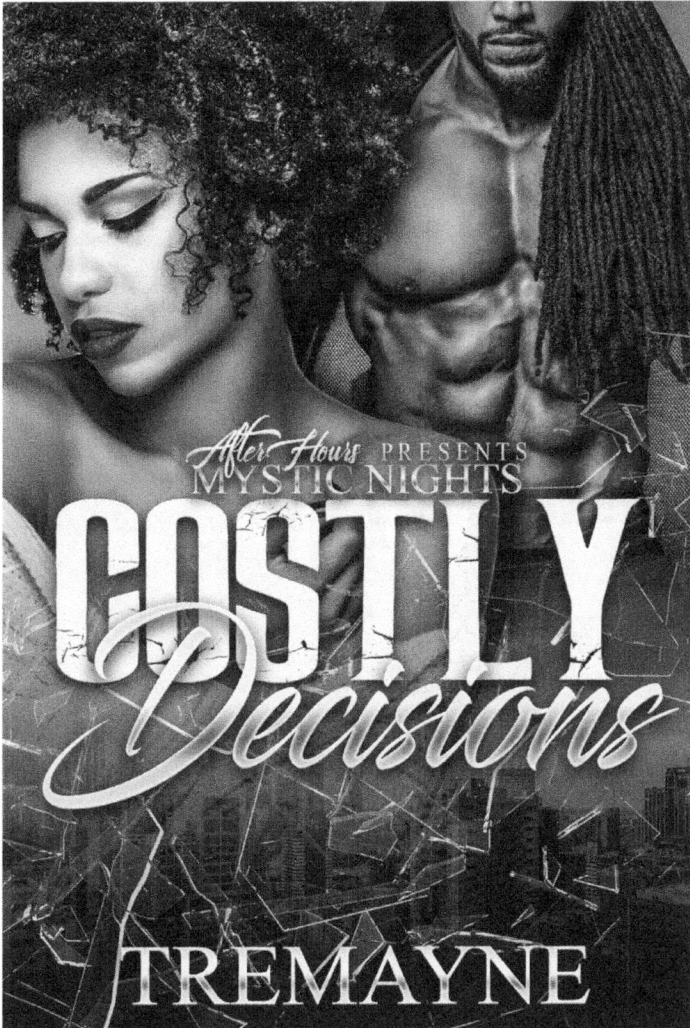

Mystic Paranormal

Mystic Young Adult

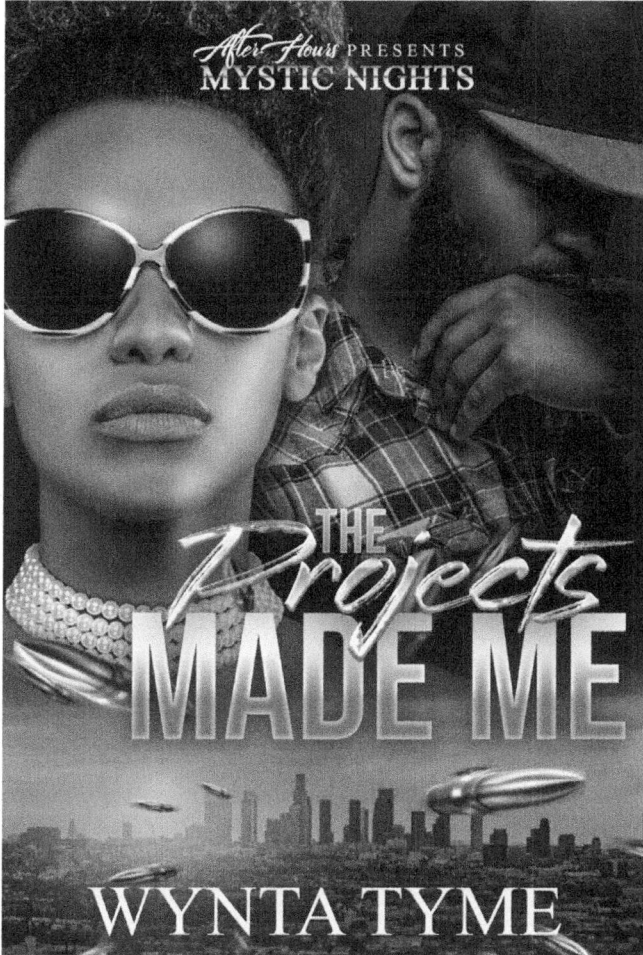

GOOD AT IT

GOOD AT IT

GOOD AT IT

After Hours PRESENTS
MYSTIC NIGHTS

GOOD AT IT

Denise WARNER

GOOD AT IT

Chapter One

I knew my mother was a career criminal by the time I was twelve. I probably should have picked up on it way earlier, but I was too busy being a kid. We had lived with my grandmother in a two-bedroom apartment in quiet, boring upstate New York until I was nine. The world was cruising into the eighties, and all I cared about was getting an Atari game system for myself.

I learned to tune out the constant bickering between my mother and grandmother. Those two chain-smoking, hot-tempered women, who locked horns over everything, were the only role models I had during my crucial developmental stages.

I know what you're thinking. Lucky me. The apartment was small. It always stunk of stale cigarettes and microwaved meals.

My grandmother was always dishing out advice that I didn't understand. She was a badass back in the day. It was written all over her face, in her mannerisms and creases, memories rarely spoken. She didn't talk about it much, but from what I gathered, she had decked a few neighborhood punks in her time.

She was a hustler from the start. She told me that she gathered apples from the neighbor's tree and sold them for cash in the schoolyard as a little girl.

As a teenager, she had a knack for window dressing and had a job at the finest department store downtown. Later, she fessed up that it allowed her to steal clothes and sell them in the poor neighborhoods, like a modern-day Robin Hood, styling the underprivileged.

My grandfather died before I was born. He was shot by police as he drove the getaway car for some thugs who had held up a corner meat and deli shop. Apparently, his thug friends were no match for the Italians who ran it.

I used to hear my mother and my grandmother, arguing over it all the time when I was little. My grandmother called him a "stupid, worthless shithead who died for eighty-five dollars," and my mother would yell back that "he was doing it to put food on the table!" It would go on for an hour back and forth, ending with my grandmother disgusted at my mother for defending him. I doubt they ever knew I was listening.

My grandmother blamed my mother for my father, leaving when I was three years old. Another contentious topic. "Your mother drove him away because she can't walk the straight and narrow, he was fed up with her schemes! It's like she learned nothing from me," she would say when my mother wasn't around. Once again, I was nine. I had no idea what she was talking about. The "straight and narrow" was a tightrope in my mind. Who could walk on that? I didn't get it.

One day, I came home from school, and my mother had our suitcases packed by the door. My grandmother was dishing out a bowl of lukewarm Spaghetti-o's at the table for me. She told me I had better eat up because my mother "fucked up, royally, and we had to leave town." I didn't know what blackmailing was, but apparently, my mother had done it to a local councilor.

My mother hushed Grandma, as she stuffed last minute things into our bags. "Come on, hurry up, eat," my mother ordered me. "Is Grandma coming?" I asked. "Not this time, Carrie," my mother started to explain, but my grandmother cut her off, "No, baby. Grandma is staying behind to clean up Roseanne's mess," she said, stubbing out a cigarette in the ashtray, next to my bowl, while shooting my mother a look.

When I was eleven, after moving two more times with my mother, once to Pennsylvania and once to Maryland, we eventually settled in Margate, Florida. My mother had us on the run again, this time because she said she was being accused of running a scam at an old folk's home where she'd taken a part-time job. My mother always used the word "accused" when she'd explain why we were driving down the highway in the middle of the night with our bags thrown in the backseat. I asked her what 'accused' meant once, and she told it was when someone "lies about you."

"Where are we going now, Mom?" I asked, pissed off because it was a week before the new school year was starting and I would never again see the friends I had made over the summer. "Florida, baby!" she announced, happily, as she flicked her cigarette ashes out the driver's side window.

GOOD AT IT

She told me that Florida was going to be great "because Mickey Mouse lived there, and we would never need winter clothes again." Even at the age of eleven, I knew I had to be cautious when it came to believing my mother. It was about that time that I had started piecing together that she was nothing like other kids' Moms. She certainly was nothing like the TV mothers I watched every night. She was no Mrs. Cunningham from "Happy Days", that's for sure. She wasn't up at the crack of dawn, packing my school lunch, nor making me a healthy breakfast.

She was usually hung over, shuffling out of the bedroom, in a robe, lighting a Virginia Slim cigarette and rummaging around her pockets for a few dollar bills for me, so I had lunch money. I had taken it upon myself to set an alarm, get up, washed, dressed for school, and have peanut butter toast or cereal before the bus came. I found solace in the routines I created for myself. It was my own form of stability.

My mother liked Florida. I was on the fence about the heat, always complaining that it was too hot all the time and whining about not having a pool at the house we were renting. My mother was usually preoccupied with studying her race forms, picking horses to bet on at the Pompano

Racetrack or sketching weird drawings of stores in plazas, which I would learn, much later, were "schematics" or layouts of the places she was going to burgle. Sometimes, at night, after I went to bed, I could hear the voices of old men she was dating on and off. I almost always fell asleep listening to the radio. I didn't question much. I missed having my grandmother around, but we'd talk on the phone, and she'd still give me gangster advice, like "Keep your nose out of trouble," and "Fly under the radar," while her television set blared "Dynasty" or "Dallas" in the background.

Chapter Two

Over the next four years, while we were in Margate, I managed to relax a little and make two good friends at school, Michelle Matthews and Bobby Ramirez. Michelle's family owned "Mattie's Florist", a large flower shop in the same plaza where Bobby's family had a mini-mart, or as they called it, a 'bodega'. Spanish was all new to me.

All during our middle school years, the three of us would hang out at that strip plaza, drinking free frozen drinks called "Parrot Ice" from the machine at Bodega Bobby's store and sit under the shady awning of the flower shop on our bikes with nothing else to do.

We were good kids, not really looking for trouble, just mainly passing the time before we had to go home to do our homework and have dinner. For me, that meant exploring a newfound passion for cooking, thanks to the cooking segments on morning TV shows. I loved them. My mother always left me money to shop for groceries so I could "play" in the kitchen. I think she felt like it kept me busy and out of her hair or from asking too many questions.

Sometimes, on weekends, she would take me to this poor excuse for a local Farmer's Market and let me pick out fruit and vegetables. She would follow behind me, talking on her massive, brick-shaped cell phone, making sure that everyone noticed she had one; they were rare back then. She would peel off dollar bills and pay for whatever I had in my hand, with a cigarette dangling from her lips and the phone cradled between her neck and shoulder, not paying attention to what I was buying. She would eat anything I made, though, even if it were bad. One time, I used rosemary instead of oregano in meatballs, and when she took a bite, her eyes went wide, but she nodded and said, "Mmm, flowery." When I bit into mine, I spat it out and angrily lectured her on being honest with me about my food. I was thirteen at the time and took my chef skills seriously.

GOOD AT IT

At the time, she was "working", by selling Amway cleaning products, for some cockamamie pyramid scheme that kept our garage full of boxes of stupid spray bottles. It never dawned on me that we had money, more than what anyone would make selling that bogus shit.

The house we rented was nice yet modest. My mother was never too flashy with money. She had slowly, over time, upgraded our car, our furnishings and I had the cool Huffy racing bicycle, and nice, new clothes and sneakers whenever I asked for them. There were certain things she stood firm on: no pets and no pool. She would just say, "Go swim at your friend's house," and that was the end of the discussion. When I'd ask for a puppy or a kitty, she would tell me that the yard was full of Gecko lizards and that I should just make those my pets because she wouldn't be cleaning up poo or pee or fur balls from any inside pets.

So, when Michelle's family bought a new house with a pool, the three of us would swim there and the bodega cat at the Ramirez's store, I thought of as my own. He had no name, so I called him Sonny Crockett because I loved "Miami

Vice". He was mainly there to keep any rats away, but any chance I'd get to feed him, pet him, or play with him, I would take it. It's funny how, as a kid, if there was a void to fill and the answer was "no", I would find some unconventional way to fill it without even noticing.

As crazy as my mother had made our life with the constant relocating, the weird hours she kept and all that, I, in turn, would find a way to normalize it. If she had extra money for things, I'd tell myself she had a good week. If she was being all hushy on the phone, I'd tell myself it was just business. I learned not to ask questions because I knew my mother wasn't ever going to tell me anything about what she was up to. It became effortless. There were times where I just didn't care. She was wacky and carefree, but I ignored it. I was uptight and always full of anxiety on the inside but didn't recognize what it was because I was busy trying to be normal.

Now I realize it was all part of the bigger act to keep anyone from asking me questions I didn't want to answer. I got away with it for years, too. I would just say she was in "sales", or that she was a businesswoman. It wasn't until I was fifteen, and Michelle, Bobby and I were walking to science class when out of nowhere, this girl

Susie Wolmack, pointed at me and yelled "Carrie Thompson's mother swindled money from my Uncle! Her Mom is a scam artist!" Everyone stopped and looked. I didn't know what to do. She just kept yelling and pointing, "Her mother is a criminal!" Susie's friends were laughing. It felt like all the normal noise of hallway chatter had stopped, and her voice was all anyone could hear. I dropped my books and charged Susie, knocking her down, and punching her, until I felt the hand of a teacher grab my arm and pull me up, yanking me to Principal Meyer's office.

It was a long wait for my mother to arrive. God only knows what the odds were that the school would call and catch my Mom at home and not at the racetrack.

I heard the doors being barged open when she arrived. My mother marched up to me, as I sat outside Mr. Meyers' door, and asked me what happened. I told her that some girl said she swindled money from her uncle and said she was a criminal, so I hit the girl.

Before I could finish my account, Mr. Meyers opened his door and called us in. I don't remember too much about what was said in the office, but I remember my mother turned the tables on Principal Meyers so fast that the poor bastard had no idea what was happening. She was spitting out words like "libel", "slander", "lawsuit", "no proof", "gossip" and of course, "accuse". By the time my mother was shoving me out the door, Mr. Meyers was apologizing to her and explaining that my three-day suspension was based on the school handbook's zero tolerance policy for violence. My mother never looked back at him, held up her middle finger, and yelled, "Where's your policy for students throwing around libelous accusations, huh? Let's get that in your fucking handbook, Meyer!"

The drive home that day was quiet. My mother chain-smoked Virginia Slims. "Is it true?" I asked. She took a long drag from her cigarette. "Listen. Number one: that little bitch has no right shoving her nose in grown-up business and b, she's got no proof, so throwing around accusations isn't in anyone's best interest." That was my mother's attempt at answering my question. I swear she could quote "L.A. Law" to the point where you'd think she's been to law school. But this time, it just didn't cut it for me. "But, Mom, is it true? Did you scam money off her Uncle?" She smacked the steering wheel and yelled, "He invested in my company! End of story!"

I rolled my eyes. So, it was true. "You never tell me anything!" I snapped. "That is my way of protecting you!" she yelled. "What you don't know can't hurt you. Get it? If you don't know anything, no one can get anything out of you. It keeps you safe. Now, knock it off." I sighed, loudly, and shook my head in disapproval. I shifted my weight and leaned against the door, staring out the window. My mother changed her tone and decided this was a teaching moment. "Look, there's some lessons to be had here. Okay? Some advice you can take with you for your whole life. A: if you're going to hit someone, make sure you knock them the fuck out, and two: never have any witnesses. Oh, and a third: always stand up for yourself and your family". I rolled my eyes at her and went back to looking out the window.

"Listen, Kiddo, you did that. So, you were on the right track. You were defending my honor, and that's great," she said, patting my leg. "... but you had a hallway full of witnesses. You should be smarter than that. Two out of three is a start, Carrie. We'll get you there, I'll teach you to build the right instincts." She was not a graduate of the Claire Huxtable School parenting by any stretch of the imagination.

The next three days sucked. I was stuck going with my mother to Pompano Race Track. She would load me up with quarters to play arcade games, buy sodas and French fries like it was some kind of "Take Your Kid to Work" day. I was bored, I was restless. I missed my friends. It was the late 80's, and my mother thoroughly looked the part. She always had that air about her, as if she just stepped out of an MTV video: big hair, tight jeans, high heels, bangle bracelets, off the shoulder blouses, her Wayfarer sunglasses and bright lipstick. She would have made Madonna proud. She had really perfected her pop star diva look. Yet I, on the other hand, had fully embraced my inner tomboy and morphed into Kristy McNichol with my board shorts, Nikes, tank top and feathered hair.

It drove my mother nuts that I didn't want to go clothes shopping, get my hair crimped, or ears pierced, and she hated my Joan Jett and Pat Benatar posters hanging all over my bedroom walls. She just couldn't understand why I wasn't into idolizing 'Blossom' and Debbie Gibson. I did think "Jo" from 'The Facts of Life' was the bomb, though. Yet, my mother wanted a daughter like "Blair".

She would bring home big black hats and plunk them down on my head and tell me, "Everyone is wearing them! Even Boy George!" I would take it off and later find her wearing it with acid washed jeans, white ruffle shirt and suspenders. She never looked her age. She never fit in with the other Moms anywhere. She was always the first to confront anyone who stared at her. "What are you looking at?" was all she had to say, and the other Moms, wherever we were - school, the grocery store, the mall - would jaunt off, in their white Capri pants, slip on shoes and sweaters tied around their shoulders.

"Listen, Care, I managed to swing a day off. It's your last day of suspension, whattaya say we do something fun, huh? A super fun day...of fun! That's what we'll call it!" "It's seven- thirty a.m., Mom," I said, from the couch.

She shoved the phone in my face. "Here, call your friends, tell them we're going to a movie today,"

I pushed the phone away. "I can't call them, they're probably at the bus stop already."

"Okay. So, let's go get them," she said, matter of factly.

GOOD AT IT

Yes, okay, sometimes, my Mom was cool when she wasn't committing a crime or embarrassing me. So, we hopped in her Camaro and off we went to 'rescue' Michelle and Bobby from a day of required high school education.

We rolled up at the bus stop where Bobby and Michelle were and yelled for them to get in the car, causing the other kids massive amounts of jealousy. We went to a Denny's and had gross, greasy, oversized breakfast platters. In true Roseanne Thompson form, we broke into a miniature golf course and played a few rounds of putt-putt before it opened, much to our delight. My mother even swiped a little pink golf ball to commemorate the day. Later we went to a matinee of "St. Elmo's Fire" at the cinema. We sang the theme song from the soundtrack cassette at the top of our lungs in the car afterward. It was a quintessential movie montage afternoon only it had happened in real life.

Then, I caught my mother checking her watch, followed by a U-turn. "Alright, kids, I have a little favor to ask before our super day of fun is over," my mother announced. I had noticed she was checking her watch all day, but I'd ignored it before because we were all having so much fun.

GOOD AT IT

She pulled into our driveway, parked the car and got out, opening the garage door. "I need everyone to grab a box or two from this pile and put it in the trunk. I'm running late for an appointment." Michelle, Bobby, myself, and my mother all grabbed a box from the carefully stacked cardboard boxes my mother had lined up along the wall of the garage. "What's in here, Mrs. T?" Bodega Bobby asked, lifting a box. Michelle had flipped back a flap on the box to see. My mother covered Michelle's hand, stopping her and tucked the flap back. "The cleaning products I sell, that's all," she said, leading Michelle to the car. My mother counted the eight boxes. Two wouldn't fit in the trunk, and Bobby and Michelle had to keep them on their laps. "I've got a buyer...a client... who needs these, and we're going to drop them off."

After driving for a short time, with my mother lowering the radio volume and following proper road rules, we pulled off into an industrial area with warehouses. My mother slowed down, looking for a certain bay number. Once she found it, she pulled up, parked the car, and opened her door. We got out and waited for my mother to give further instructions as she opened the trunk.

"Okay, everybody, grab a box and unload it over there," she pointed to an area by the warehouse door. We hustled, stacking the boxes outside the door. She rang a buzzer a few times and waited, looking at her watch again. Bobby and I walked around to the trunk again. Michelle was putting the boxes in the area my mother pointed out. As Bobby pulled the last box out, the bottom gave way, and everything began spilling out into the trunk.

There were ziplock baggies of jewelry, mostly watches, all packed underneath the bottles of cleaning products. Bobbie's mouth dropped opened. "Oh, for fuck's sake," I muttered as I hurriedly fixed the box flaps and began shoving everything back in. Bobby didn't say a word as Michelle walked up. "Come on, you guys quit fooling ar-" Her eyes locked onto the remaining baggies in the trunk. She looked at me, then back at the stuff in a panic. She pointed at one of the bags. It was filled with pot. "Jesus Christ! Is that weed? Wait, ...and...watches? Holy shit!" She picked up a bag and looked at it. Bobby yanked it from her hand and stuffed in the box. "Shhh, shut up!" he said. It was like he was already a pro at this, probably something to do with his cousins being gang members and hanging around the dodgy cliental of the bodega.

I was sweating and peeked around the trunk to see my mother talking to what looked like, one big, badass biker dude with a bunch of tattoos and bushy beard and ponytail. He was counting a wad of money into my mother's hand as they spoke in hushed tones. "Get this back in the box!" I whispered harshly. We put the rest of the baggies back in and started putting the bottles of cleaner on top. "Wait, wait!" Bobby said, before putting the last bottle back on top of a bag of stash. He quickly pinched a big bud from the weed bag and zipped the baggie back up. He shoved the bud in his pocket, grinning like a fool. "Party later," he said, smiling. "Hurry up!" I hissed at him. We crushed everything back in, closed it up, and I put the box with the others. Bobby slammed the trunk closed, and we all got in the car as my mother finished her "business transaction." I was so embarrassed. I could feel my face getting redder beneath the layer of sweat. Bobby was happy. Michelle was mortified. I was devastated. My mother? Delighted. She got back in the car, tucking the cash into her purse on the seat. She handed us each a ten-dollar bill. "Here you go for helping me. Now, who wants pizza?" she asked, adjusting her sunglasses in the rear-view mirror. My heart was beating a mile a minute as I turned to face the window in my usual huff. I pointed the air conditioning vents on myself and ignored my mother. "I could eat," Bobby said, happily from the back seat, as if nothing had happened. Michelle and I made eye contact, me looking in the side mirror and her looking right back at me, bewildered.

After gorging on under-cooked, sloppy pizza, my mother dropped us off behind the bodega. As we got out of the car and walked around it, Bobby leaned in and gave my mother a kiss on the cheek. "Thanks for the super fun day of fun, Mrs. T. Maybe Carrie could punch Susie Wolmack in the face again next week." My mother laughed as she looked right past him at the back door to the bodega. I saw her eyes fixate on the security light, and then the alarm panel box. Michelle thanked my Mom, and she and Bobby headed to the door. "I'll be right there," I said, before leaning in the driver's side window, as if I was kissing my mother good-bye, too but I put my mouth close to her ear. "If you even think about robbing this place, I will burn the rest of your garage boxes in a massive bonfire, got it?"

My mother's eyes widened, and loudly, she said, "I had fun, too. You're welcome, darling!" "Mom, I mean it," I snapped.

She lowered her sunglasses to make eye contact with me, "Carrie, don't be silly. I'm not your grandfather. I'm not interested in places that make eighty-five dollars a day." With that remark, she drove off. My fists were clenched. I exhaled and turned towards Bobby and Michelle, who were waiting for me by the back door. I put on my happy face and stifled my anger. Bobby had swiped a pack of Zig-Zag rolling papers from the store and managed to roll three little joints from that bud of weed he nicked from the baggie. The three of us got high every night that weekend.

I fessed up about my mother to them as we sat by Michelle's pool while her parents were out for the evening. Michelle's mouth hung open. Bobby loved the excitement of it all. I told them how much it bugged me that my Mom wasn't like normal Moms. After telling me I was lucky to have such a cool Mom, Bobby fell asleep on a lounge chair. Michelle and I sat on the edge of the pool with our feet in the water. I purged my innermost thoughts about my life, even telling her about my grandfather. I told her how I was sick of living in fear that the police would show up and take my mother away or worse yet, shoot her in some heist gone wrong. God knows, my mother wouldn't go down without a fight. Michelle listened intently, and hugged me, not judging me at all.

I shared my hopes of going to culinary school and working at some glamorous place in California like "The Ivy", serving up meals to Hollywood's elite, far away from my family and their shitty history.

She quietly told me that she couldn't wait to get away, either. Her parents reveled in putting pressure on her to get good grades and go to college, it was all about keeping up appearances to them, and no child of theirs was going to be slacker.

"But what do you want to do?" I asked her. "I just want to slack," she laughed. "Honestly, I don't know …but I like to paint and draw." I nodded, listening to her. "I love art class," she stated, shyly. I should have known. Michelle was always sketching and doodling. Her mother had allowed her to paint a mural on the bedroom wall, which was a stunning fairy forest scene and she added fairy lights to it, making it come alive when turned off her bedroom light. I sniffled away the snot and wiped my tears.

"Then you'll be a famous artist, and I'll be a famous chef." She smiled, squeezed my hand, then quickly leaned in, and kissed me. I didn't know I was a lesbian until pretty much that very moment. I mean, I knew I liked girls way better than boys, but I wasn't sure what to make of it. I sure as hell didn't know Michelle felt the same way. I remember thinking her kissing me was the best feeling ever. It surprised me how we just fell right into it as if we had been kissing forever. We fit together so perfectly. It was almost innocent, yet taboo, but it was us, and it felt right. We made out for an entire hour, no grinding, no rushing for more, just literally savoring how amazing it felt …until Bobby stirred awake, asking for Fritos and a Coke.

***

It was a month after school let out. I was working part-time at my first ever job, at an ice cream kiosk in the mall. Michelle had a job at a record store a few spaces down from where I worked. Bobby was successfully selling weed to the stoner crowd that hung out at the food court, so we were basically having the summer of our lives together. I can remember so clearly Michelle and I getting off work, gathering Bobby and watching the Live-Aid concert on television at my house for the entire fifteen hours, recording our favorite acts on VHS and watching them on repeat next day. We were completely oblivious to the real world. But we were all about this noble gesture by Bob Geldof to raise money for starving Ethiopians.

We didn't know anything about Reagan meeting with Gorbachev, we didn't know about Terry Anderson being kidnapped in Beirut, we didn't know about the hijacking of TWA Flight 847, we didn't know about Boris Becker winning Wimbledon at the age of seventeen. All we knew were MTV, Nintendo, "We Are The World", and that Coca-Cola had introduced a new product called "Cherry Coke". The important things to know when you're sixteen.

Michelle was excited that the mall was having an art show with two of her painting chosen to be in it. Bobby was higher than a kite all the time. He spent every spare dollar on tattoos. I was getting braver in the kitchen, even learning to make my own honey mustard dip and dressing with this new mustard I discovered called Dijon. My mother was still eating whatever I made, always being supportive, except when I served undercooked chicken. She obviously drew the line of support at contracting food poisoning.

Michelle and I got our driver's licenses at the same time. My mother was giving me shit about buying me my own car. "Not happening," she would end the conversation with those two words, no matter how much I pleaded. Bobby had failed his road test twice. His older brother would let him borrow his car once in a while during the day, but we were desperate to go cruising down the Fort Lauderdale strip at night. Michelle had the brilliant idea that she would offer to do some flower deliveries for her parents, and we would get a spare car key made at the mall for the van. She would hide the key in a magnetic box under the wheel well, and almost every night, we'd ride our bikes to the plaza, and take the van cruising. Like I said, best summer ever. On the nights when Bobby would blow us off to go out with his stoner friends, we would spend hours making out in the van, grinding on each other, getting one another off, breathless and sweaty.

Even when we were back at school, we never talked about being a couple or what was happening, though. It was between us and only happened in the van or on weekend sleepovers.

Other nights, when Bobby would hang out with us, we would drive to Pompano Pier, listen to music, then cruise down A1A along the beach, into Fort Lauderdale, past all the iconic bars like The Elbo Room and The Candy Store, hooting and hollering out of the windows at the drunken partiers. Every April when the Spring Breaker's arrived, it was like a two week, non-stop party down at the beach. It was Fort Lauderdale's claim to fame, and we had a front row seat to it.

Some nights, we sat on the beach and talked about our families and what our childhoods were like. How we saw our futures panning out. What cool apartments we'd have, what cool cars we'd have.

Some nights, I'd spend having it out with my mother over typical things, like wanting to get a fake ID to get into clubs. My mother wasn't having any of that. "At your age, you don't do things that could involve police or pregnancies!" she would yell at me. I would tell her that I was old enough to make my own decisions and that I had a job and made my own money working at the ice cream shop and one day I was going to be a famous chef, and she wouldn't be able to tell me what do. Door slam, foot stomp. The whole nine yards. We'd be upset and quiet for the rest of the night. In the morning, especially on the weekend, I'd come out in my uniform for work at the ice cream store, and I'd be complaining about how stupid it looked, she would say "so quit if you don't like it."

My mother didn't understand why I wanted to work at the age of fifteen, slinging ice cream cones for minimum wage. She thought I should be having fun. I'd argue that I couldn't have fun without a fake ID and it would start all over again. She would say, "You have your whole life to work". She'd tell me that I was going to be just like my Dad, happy to just get by, working a daily grind for peanuts so I should have a good time now while I was young. I would then leave the house with another door slam.

I firmly believed that I wasn't like either of them. I wasn't a thief like my mother, and I never left like my father did. I was nothing like either of them. I don't really know how my mother chose the life she was leading, to be honest.

I remember her once telling me how much she had hated that my Dad didn't want "the finer things in life," that he was perfectly okay with working for seven or eight dollars an hour, saving up money to buy things, and waiting for vacation days to relax. She said she hated not being able to go buy what she needed when she needed it and didn't want to live that way. She also said she didn't see that changing any time soon, back then. My mother never gave me details about anything, but she did sort of explain when it all started.

So, apparently, when I was three years old, she saw an ad in the paper about a local estate sale. She told me that she knew being "a woman with a baby was the perfect distraction". She went in, she browsed, she chatted, the estate agent cooed and giggled with me as I toddled around and she just discreetly tucked a valuable bracelet into the bag hanging off my stroller. She made small talk while gathering me up and making an excuse to leave, and confidently walked out of the place. She then fenced it at a pawn shop one city over and got a "huge wad of cash", as she put it. "It was more than the 'allotted weekly allowance' your father would give me, I'll tell you that much!" she boasted, proudly. I guess there was no looking back then. She was a twenty-eight-year-old single mother and a jewel thief with no remorse. "I was good at it, Carrie! I really was!" she said, all happy with herself. My father got fed up with her games and secrecy and finally divorced her around that time. I seriously don't think she cared because she had decided on the life she wanted, she was excited about it, and it was way better than what my father had in mind. She never appeared to have any regrets.

My father moved to Colorado soon after the divorce and would send birthday cards every year. He never once invited me out there or dared to cross my mother by asking her if I could visit. I basically forgot all about him until a card showed up. Even then, as I got older, I didn't miss the idea of having a Dad around like I did when I was younger and I'd hear kids at school talking about Daddy this and Daddy that. I guess as we get older, we find other things to talk about because our parents aren't as cool as lip gloss and cassette tapes and hair bands.

When I would talk to Michelle or Bobby about my home life, I'd leave out certain details, like that whole 'Mom's a jewel thief thing' or how I felt about my Dad's absence but one thing was for sure, we all had our family strife, and I'm sure that was part of what bonded us. The other part was just that we all really liked and cared about each other. Our dynamic was the thing we were all missing, and it held us together.

My senior year of high school seemed to fly by. Everyone was getting serious about their next moves. The nerds were prepping and taking SAT tests for college, jobs were being lined up, homecoming and prom were a constant buzz. Bobby, Michelle, and I threw an Anti-Prom beach party for those not willing to partake in that stupid, expensive, time-honored tradition, and it was an unexpected hit. We had band geeks, the chess club, the Dungeons & Dragon weirdos and the quiet invisibles show up with food and beer, and oddly enough, we all had a blast. No one made fun of anyone, we all fit in for a moment in time, realizing that we had more in common than we thought.

We cooked burgers on charcoal grills, drank wine coolers and beers, and laughed a lot, talking about elementary and middle school years, teachers and other students. We had a boom box playing 80's pop and rock, blankets on the sand, some played cards, some played a few rounds of Spin-the-Bottle, everyone did their own thing and felt like they belonged. At times, we'd hear the beeping horns of limousines and shrieks from our classmates cruising to the prom host hotel, and we'd just flip our middle fingers up and take a swig like a drinking game. I don't know if it was because the drinks were flowing, or we were just feeling...safe, but it was the first time Michelle, and I held hands and snuggled together in front of anyone. It didn't seem to faze anyone. We stayed until the wee hours and eventually packed up our crap and headed home at the break of dawn with pounding headaches and approaching hangovers. The sign of a good night. Michelle drove us home in the flower delivery van, which she now had permission to use, stopping at a McDonald's drive-through for breakfast. We dropped Bobby off with his giant bag of food and headed next to my house. The sun was up by now, our hangovers coming into full bloom; we had on our dark sunglasses, hair in floppy ponytails and big hoodie shirts on to stay warm in the cool morning air. I groaned as we turned down my street.

"No joke, I'm going to sleep until dinner time, and then some," I stated.

"Same," Michelle said, as we rolled up to my house. I gathered my things, still holding my McDonald's Egg McMuffin, which I was already eating. Michelle gave me a nudge. "Hey, who is that in the driveway?" I looked up to see a man, leaning against a car I didn't recognize that had a rental sticker on it. I squinted behind my shades. "Jesus Christ," I murmured. "What?" Michelle asked, looking at him then back to me.

"Oh my God," she gasped, "Is that …?" I sighed heavily and handed her my egg McMuffin. "My father. Here. I just lost my appetite." I opened the van door and got out. "Wait, Carrie," she said, with a mouthful of breakfast sandwich, "do you want me to stay?"

"Nah. I got this," I replied, slinging my beach bag over my shoulder, gripping my McDonald's Coke. I made my way up the driveway as Michelle slowly drove away a few feet. Then she stopped and yelled to me out of the window, "I'm just gonna stay right here for now!" Maybe we had watched too much "Cagney & Lacey," but Michelle was going to have herself a little stakeout in case my father tried abducting a seventeen-year-old me or something. I gave her a quick thumbs-up as she parked a few houses down and turned the engine off.

My father had attempted to establish some form of a relationship with me over the years, through random awkward phone messages on the answering machine, holiday cards and short "Hope you're well" postcards but I just literally didn't give a shit. I mean, I read them, but I had absolutely no thoughts whatsoever, and I didn't have it in me to fake it, so I just ignored them. Half the time, when he'd call, if he did manage to catch me at home, I'd tell my mother to say I wasn't there. The other times, I'd listen a bit, say "yeah", "cool", "really" and then usually end the conversation by saying, "I have to go. Mom's calling me," when she wasn't even there at the time. Part of me tried to be happy that he was even thinking about me, trying to make a connection, but a bigger part resented him for leaving. Not that he left ME so much as he left my Mom and although she never for one second showed any hurt over it, I knew that at some point my father was the love of her life or she wouldn't have married him. It took me a while to get it, but it became more apparent to me as the years went on and she didn't really ever commit to anyone or have a steady boyfriend. She had been so hurt by his leaving, and she wasn't going to risk it again. I firmly believed that my mother, over the years, talked herself into being "glad he was gone" and that's why she always presented it as she "was better off", and she could "do her own thing", and he "was a loser with a minimum wage job" and all that sort of stuff. Perhaps it was for my benefit, so I didn't know she was sad. But, the more I grew up, the more I understood it, and eventually, I felt nothing towards him.

GOOD AT IT

When I was nine, we got flyers to bring home about a "Father & Daughter Dance" at school. I went into the house, and I threw out a lot of pictures I had of him because I hated that feeling of missing him and pictures made it worse. My mother was really upset by it but told me it was my choice to trash my pictures, and I'd likely regret it. She also firmly warned me not to touch her photo albums or pictures, or she'd bust my fingers. Her feelings toward him varied. When he first left, I used to hear them argue on the phone over him wanting to talk to me, and her not letting him, but I was way too young to understand it. Over the years, they had established a weird non-invasive friendship, I guess. He'd call, she'd update him on me, it wouldn't be long conversations, but the anger was gone. At some point, she must have felt that her protecting me from the same potential hurt she had felt long ago was getting in the way of any sort of potential relationship I might have with him. What if once again he dropped off the face of the earth, how damaging it would be for me? But she did what she thought was right and was cautious about it.

I remember we seemed to talk a bit more about him once I was a teenager. I was fourteen and a half when my mother finally eased into it. She sat me down and asked if I wanted to talk to him, she said it was my decision. He wanted to re-connect. She wasn't forcing me to or not to. Like any angst-ridden teen, I shrugged and said, "I don't care. Whatever. No big whoop." She said, "I think maybe you should." So, I did. I remember during the first few calls it bothered me that I struggled to remember his face while he was yammering on about the mountains in Colorado. Now here he was. Standing there, pasty pale, looking kind of like a weathered, old Matt Dillon, in tan Bermuda shorts, a god awful, loose, bright Hawaiian shirt and goofy Dad sneakers with no socks. He was beaming at me. I was tired, hungover, and not chipper in the least. I half-heartedly waved a lame, limp wave, now standing before him.

"Mom wouldn't let you in?" I ask as I shield the strong sun with my hand.

"No, she did. Even had a cup of coffee with her. But it…ahh…well…It felt a little forced and um…maybe a bit awkward. So, I decided to wait out here. Get some rays, some fresh air, read the paper…" he waved the folded sports section of the Sun-Sentinel that he had tucked under his arm. I leaned on the car bumper next to him, not looking directly at him.

I was already over his peppiness. "What are you doing here, Dad?' I said, taking a sip of my Coke, looking down at my tanned feet in my flip flops. His big smile faded a bit at my reaction, but he kept a positive tone.

"Well, you're graduating soon, that's a big deal. I wanted to be there, but I just can't get those dates off from work. This was the only time I could come. I wanted to see you...you're older now, growing up fast, making all kinds of decisions about the future and whatnot...."

I nodded my head and chewed on my straw, giving him a sideways glance.

"I've missed out on a lot, Carrie. I haven't been a presence in your life...hardly ever...and certainly not at any of the important times, and I don't want that to be the case anymore."

I could feel him staring at me, waiting for a response. For the life of me, I could not help myself, and I busted out laughing. Wiping my Coke dribble off my lip, setting my beach bag down on the driveway, bent over, literally laughing out loud. I push my sunglasses up into my hair. "Oh, Jesus, Dad. I'm sorry, but come on. 'I don't want that to be the case anymore'..." I imitated, with a sigh, shaking my head. "Yeah. You HAVE missed out on a lot. My first day of school, my first A plus on my report card, boogers, chicken pox, ceramic ashtrays, my first fight, my first suspension, my first attempt at pancakes, epic fail by the way, my first boy crush, my first girl crush, my first cramps, my first period, and here we are now with high school pretty much over - I mean what... a... bummer FOR YOU."

"Carrie, I know it's been hard on you. Of course, I know that. Wait, did you say 'girl crush'?" I nodded, and motioned to Michelle, still parked across the street in the van, keeping an eye on me. She slid her sunglasses down her nose as my Dad looked over at her. He scratched his chin, "Well, um...okay. Errr...Cool." He got himself back on track, "Um, honey, I know that I made bad choices because I didn't know how to handle things. I didn't want to upset you or your mother. I should have tried harder. I took the easy way out, and I stayed away. I could have tried sooner and harder ...and I didn't."

"Well, guess what? It worked for me."

"Okay. I hear you. But things are different now. WE'RE different now. All of us. Me, your Mom, you...Look, I know I made a ton of mistakes, but I've been doing a lot of thinking lately, and I'd really like it if you came out to

Colorado. Maybe look at some colleges out there, you could live me, let me try and make up for it, ya know? We could-"

"Stop, Dad. Stop."

"What? Come on, think about it. Just think about it. That's all I'm asking."

"I don't need to. I'm fine here. Listen, me and Mom…as much as she bugs me, we're a team. And I'm sorry but…you're not on it."

"Carrie, the life your mother leads, it's not good. Don't you ever stop and wonder what would happen if she ever got caught in one of her scams or heists or whatever it is she does? She could end up in jail at any moment. Then what? What happens to you?"

"NOW you're worried about that? NOW? When I'm old enough to take care of myself? What the fuck, Dad?" I instinctively hit him in the arm.

"I know what it sounds like! But back then, I couldn't have been able to care for you, I was barely getting by on my salary. I was always worried about that. About getting 'the call'…my God. I couldn't have raised you on my own back then. Now, though, you're older. If she gets caught, the implications are more serious for you. Carrie, things are good with me. I have a good job, I make good money. I have a house…in the mountains…," His voice trailed off as he watched me, thinking.

I lowered my voice back to normal, I looked at him, finally. "You know, Mom could have left me with Grandma at any time. She always had that choice. But she didn't. Ever. I was her responsibility, and she knew it, and unlike you, she never left. She was there for the chicken pox and the report cards and the cramps and the crushes. So, no matter what she does for a living, whether it's stupid, or dangerous, she's good at it. And here I am, with her, we're together, and I'm fine. So, whatever you had in mind with this big grand gesture, whatever you thought was going to happen here today, it's just not… I'm sorry, but it's not. Okay?"

"You won't even please just think about it?"

"No, I won't. I'm happy here. Trust me, Dad, that wasn't always the way, but it is now. I have Mom, and good friends, a girlfriend, a job, plans. I'm not leaving all that. Look, I get it. You hit a certain age, and you're all like 'Oh, I need to be a better Dad' or whatever, but it's not what I need. What I need is for things to go back the way they were. You're a guy with a daughter, I'm a girl with a father, and maybe we'll get to know each other better in time, but for me, that time isn't right now."

He nodded his head, letting the words sink in. He folded his arms across his chest, leaning against the car bumper, looking down at the ground. I did the same. The silence was longer than I expected. I didn't have any words left, quite honestly.

"I'll tell you what. Your Mom must be doing something right because you're pretty smart, you know that?" He paused for a second. "You are correct. I made this about me, I shouldn't have, and for that, I apologize. But I won't apologize for trying. I know, it'll probably drive you nuts, but I'm not going to stop trying to be better. Maybe...down the line, in the future, we can know each other more. Get to a place where it's not weird. What do you think?"

"You'll have to lose that shirt first."

He laughed a little. "Deal."

He extended his hand to shake mine, but I know he really wanted a hug. He didn't push it. He didn't get it. He got the handshake, with an honest smile.

"I'm sorry you came all the way out here for this," I said, "we probably could have had this conversation on the phone."

"It's okay. Truth is, I wanted to see your face. I don't really have any good pictures of us, and I didn't want to forget what you look like. So, I came to see you. See your pretty face. I know. Selfish."

"No. No, I get that one. I really do," I said, remembering that feeling of being on the phone with him, not being able to picture his face.

"Sounds stupid, but listen…you be good. Look after your Mom. Take care of yourself." He made his way to the car door.

"It's not stupid. I'll send you some graduation pictures." I vowed. And I meant it.

'I'd like that. Very much."

I picked up my bag and walked along the other side of the car, glancing over the top for a second to catch him staring at me, smiling but getting teary-eyed. Almost like he didn't want to go for a moment.

"Don't make it weird, Dad," I said, laughing a little.

"Okay!" He laughed, "I get it. I get it. I'll call you soon," he said, getting in the car and starting it. He waved as he backed out of the driveway, wiping his face. I watched him leave. This time, it's not so bad.

I stood there for a second before Michelle beeped the horn and scared me back into the moment. "Dude! Ya okay?" She yelled from the window.

"I'm alright!"

"Was it weird?"

"SO weird!" I shout back, making big eyes, pulling my sunglasses back down, shaking my head.

She laughed as she drove away. I turned toward the house just as the front door opened to see my mother standing there in her drawstring pajama pants and a tank top, bathrobe hanging on her shoulders. She was barefoot, holding a mug of coffee. She leaned on the door frame as I made my way to her, and then she hugged me tightly with one arm and kissed my head. I gave her a squeeze.

The thing I loved about my mother is that it never felt like she had a super tight grip on me, like the way Michelle parents were with her. She was never holding onto me super tight, not in the literal sense like she was doing in the doorway at that moment, but in a metaphoric sense. She didn't ignore me the way Bobby's parents inadvertently did with him because of a brood of siblings and full-time jobs. My mother gave me space, she allowed me to be free, be independent, but she was never far away or out of reach, and she certainly could have been a complete hoverer given her past relationship with my Dad. She could have been smothering me, always worried that I'd run away, go be with him or my grandmother, or skip out and crash with friends or something, but I got the sense that she just trusted I wouldn't leave. Like I trusted she wouldn't. It was unspoken, hardly ever noticed but in that minute, I felt it. My mother probably knew what my father was going to ask, maybe he told her, and that's why it became awkward over coffee. But my mother knew I wasn't going anywhere and that doorway hug indicated that. I sighed heavily into her bathrobe. "What the hell?" I yelled into her fuzzy collar. She giggled a bit. "How's that for a hangover?" she said in my ear.

"I need to sleep!" I said, untangling myself from her.

"What sleep? I want one of your famous spinach omelets!" she said, following me in the house.

"You get a simple cheese, and that's it, I'm exhausted!" I teased.

<u>Chapter Three</u>

Over the next few days, I filled Michelle in on whatever she couldn't overhear being parked across the road, and she kept saying how amazed she was at how good I was handling all this "Dad shit", as she called it. I didn't really know what she was talking about because, as I stated to her, "I can't really know what I'm missing if I've never had it, though, so it's not that big of a deal." "Fair enough," she said. We filled Bobby in about the whole thing a few weeks later while we were on our way up to Orlando. We had all saved up enough money to do a weekend at Disney World. We got a cheap hotel room, had Bobby's older brother's car, had gas money, a bottle of Jack Daniels, some weed and we were full of Senior Spirit as the school year was coming to an end. It was a great time. We bought Instamatic cameras and took pictures with Tigger, Pooh, Mickey, and

Minnie, we rode all the rides, laughed and ate ice cream bars in the shape of Mouse Ears. At night, we ate junk food, smoked a bit of weed, did some shots of whiskey, and listened to mix tapes on the boom box we had in the hotel room until we'd fall asleep. My mother was an essential part of the plan, because of course, Michelle parents said no to the weekend right off the bat, so we ended up having to tell them she was staying at my house and then we asked my mother to lie for us. Of course, she did it, and this time, the price was that I had to make her eggs benedict for the following two weekend mornings. I was secretly happy to cook anything for anyone, even though I'd act like it was a chore. Bobby's cousin went to Key West during lobster season, and he brought over a whole bunch of fresh lobster, so my mother let all of us have a seafood festival at our house. I did all the cooking and was in my element. She even let us have margaritas, but we all had share just one small pitcher because she said she didn't want to clean any throw up from anyone. There were times at that party I would catch my mother noticing how close Michelle and I were, but she kept it to herself. Bobby taught her some salsa dancing, and that kept her distracted enough for Michelle and I to sneak off to my room. We had a fast and furious make-out session that led to hands into shorts, that led to bodies mashing together on my desk, that led to orgasms. Flushed, and glowing, I managed to put out quite the feast.

Everyone seemed genuinely happy that whole year. So, I literally have no idea how we all grew apart so fast after graduation.

It's all a bit of a blur. My grandmother had flown to Florida to see me graduate. Michelle's parents were pissy about her not getting a scholarship but more so that she wanted to go to an art college in Fort Lauderdale. Bobby graduated by the skin of his teeth and had no real plan other than to be the Latino version of the "Fast Times At Ridgemont High" character, Jeff Spicolli. I clearly remember just wanting the day to end because my mother and grandmother were at each other's throats from the ceremony to the small party at our house afterward.

My mother gave me a car key that day. It opened her old Camaro. She had a brand, new t-top Corvette by then. She was onto bigger scores now. I always knew when something was up because she would watch the news like a hawk if they reported on a jewelry store robbery. She would bite down hard, flexing her jaw muscles until the newscaster said, "police have no known suspects at this time" at which point she would relax again. Soon after that, nice things started to appear: clothes, shoes, furniture, the Corvette. It was a pattern, and I was on to it. So, it wasn't a massive surprise that I'd get the old Camaro, once she pulled up with a new Corvette.

My grandmother stayed for a week after my graduation. She and my mother argued like the old times for the entire visit. The only time they managed to pull it together was when I cooked for them. "You've come a long way from Spaghetti-O's, Carrie," my grandmother stated proudly as I served up Cuban pork roast with garlic potatoes and plantains.

Grandma died from a heart attack two months after getting back to New York. My mother flew up there, but I stayed back because the Culinary School I'd taken a place at was starting, and I couldn't miss my orientation or classes.

For the first time, I was learning to disconnect from the chaos of my life and prioritize what I wanted to focus on - school. I felt awful about my grandmother dying but was kind of relieved that I didn't have to go up to New York with my mother. I questioned whether it was being focused or whether it was being selfish.

GOOD AT IT

My mother was mad at me about not going with her. She was gone almost a month, taking care of arrangements, fighting with the rest of the family, as usual. She would call me daily and tell me every detail, and I would do the "oh, wow," sympathy thing. She would end every conversation with "I really wish you were here, Carrie." I would try to suck it up, but finally, I shouted, "Don't make me feel guilty about this!" and hung up on her.

Later, when she got back, she confessed that she understood my choice, and she was upset because she just didn't want to fly alone. I knew that was a lie and she missed my support, but I didn't call her out on it. I didn't see the need, and I was laser focused at school.

Maybe it's because I remained so focused and driven while I was at Culinary School that I slowly lost touch with Bobby and Michelle. I don't think I even realized it was happening.

Even though we all lived in the same state, same area, not ridiculously far from where we grew up, none of us stayed in touch like we had been. All three of us were just living our post-high school lives. Michelle was in art school, Bobby was working at the bodega selling Funnyons,

Gatorade, and weed to his client base, and I was at cooking school, living with a gay roommate near the campus in Miami and working at a café on Collins Avenue.

I rarely went back to Margate to see my mother. When she did call me, the conversation was always short. I'd tell her how busy I was and that I'd call her back. I did show up for holidays and birthdays with big fancy dishes of food and pastry that I had made. I never really brought girlfriends home, out of sheer embarrassment of my Mom. She was getting flashier and raunchier with age, and she flaunted the signs of the money she was bringing in from her scams.

When I did visit, there would usually be just us and whichever random loser guy she was undoubtedly hustling at the time. They were generally underwhelmed by my cooking creations; instead, drinking and feeding each other olives and gherkin pickles off my mother's shitty appetizer plates, while calling each other stupid pet names. After a while, I stopped showing up at all. I kept busy with school and dating girls here and there, never looking for anything more than casual sex.

GOOD AT IT

I think it was in 1995 that I last made a genuine effort to see my Mom. I dragged myself to her 50th birthday party which took place at the Pompano Racetrack, so she could bet on the horses while she celebrated in the "Big Winner" Bar, which was most often full of losers. She had quite the crowd around her, seeing as she spent most of her time there. She knew all the regular patrons, and she was, as usual, the center of attention.

That day, she won big on a horse named "Care Bear" and handed me a wad of cash in front of everyone, saying she picked the horse because the name meant something to her, impressing her social circle once more. I knew better. She had done the form research or fucked a jockey for a hot tip, it wasn't just dumb luck or sentiment, as she pretended in order to charm her friends.

I don't know how much my mother won that night, but when I got home and counted the cash, there were over two thousand dollars in my pocket. She was doing well. I didn't ask how or why, I learned not to, preferring ignorance to knowing what she was up to. She was generous when she remembered to be, but I still thought it was best to limit my engagement with her. In fact, I got to the point where I had purchased a separate cheap cell phone under my roommate's name just for calling her because I didn't want to be tied to her in any way if she ever did get pinched by the cops.

I lived a different life. I was happy in the bubble I had created. My mother never understood why anyone, especially me, would want a nine to five work life, "the rat race", "the daily grind" she would call it. When I got the job at the ice cream store at the age of 15 and told her it was a stepping stone to becoming a chef someday, she told me I was just like my father, "happy to just get by." I was furious. It was comments like that from my mother that annoyed the shit out of me because she actually believed it.

Chapter Four

I got so good at disconnecting from my family that one day I woke up and realized I hadn't seen my mother in almost a decade. We talked on the phone sporadically over the years, but nothing routine. It didn't bother me, maybe because it happened slowly, over time. I told myself I had tried. My mother didn't push or whine or beg me to visit her. She had her own life. A full life. I didn't really want to know what sort of trouble it was full of.

In 2005, she was living in a gated community somewhere in Boca Raton, where a bunch of retirees hatched their nest eggs and crammed themselves full of cream cheese and lox bagels and layered meat subs. She was sixty years old.

I was thirty-five, at the height of my career, working at a hot new restaurant called "Bongo's Cuban Café" that Gloria Estefan and her husband, Emilio, had opened in Miami a few years earlier, my dream job. The place was flashy, exciting, and the crowds were huge. It was part of the Miami Arena, where Miami Heat played. The vibe was spectacular, the pay was phenomenal, and according to the reviews, the food was terrific. That was all me. The menu and the restaurant had Cuban flare. Celebrities and basketball players with their entourages came in and ate, all right in the heart of the city.

Unfortunately, the hours were long and hard, and I rarely got days off. I was doing what I loved, though, even if it meant my feet and back hurt constantly, and I never had free time to do much else other than work and sleep.

It was around then that I had a voicemail from my mother saying that she wanted me to come and see her, stressing it was important. I remember thinking she sounded old and tired. It had been a while after all.

I called her back on a quick break. We spoke briefly about where I was living and working, and not long into the conversation, she had a coughing fit, before making me promise to come see her, and then abruptly hanging up. I wasn't thrilled, but I did arrange the day off and drove north to Boca Raton a few days later.

Her development, Boca De La Cruz, was on the inter-coastal waterway, which leads to the Atlantic Ocean. I drove up to the gates where a security guard, who was as old as the residents, poked his head out. He was pleasant and politely asked who I was there to see.

"Roseanne Thompson," I stated.

"Oh! Ro? Lovely…and you are?"

"Carrie."

He went back inside, made a call and poked his head out again, "Straight through, first right, around the bend, to 1151."I drove through the community, noticing the signs of luxury living: gardeners, landscapers, pool companies, and fancy cars dotting the driveways. There were palm trees every two feet, manicured lawns, and plenty of fat, tanned, shirtless, grey-cotton ball headed men with gold chains around their necks fussing around their yards, hosing their driveways and wiping off their big metallic Cadillacs.

"Well, Mom, you finally made it. Old, rich people's utopia." I thought as I rounded the bend to her pretentious homeowner association-regulated coral-colored house, complete with a barrel tile roof, at 1151.

I parked my modest Jeep next to her shiny, new convertible Mercedes. I walked up to the double doors and rang the doorbell. I took a deep breath, prepared for the unknown. A tall, thin, Latino black guy, dressed in white shorts and a white polo shirt answered the door. He must have been in his late twenties, with a dark complexion, blinding white teeth, perfect short, curly black hair, and thick, full lips.

"Hola. Bienvenido, Mees Carrie," he said, gesturing to come in with an exaggerated Willy Wonka type of bow. "Uh...hi," I said. "Right dis way, if joo follow me," he instructed in broken English or Spanglish. With a lisp. He swirled on his tennis sneakered heel and swished through the foyer into a large, stark, glistening white kitchen with a magnificent island, tons of counter space, and the best name brand appliances. I could feel myself tighten up. He swished, once again, and gestured toward my Mom, with a weird bow, as if she was Cher, Goddess of the Gays, or something.

GOOD AT IT

"Here joo go," he said, and he sashayed toward the table. "Oh my god," I thought. "If RuPaul and Charo had a son, he'd be it."

Yep, we have a queen here, I noted to myself, and it wasn't my mother, for once. My mother was sitting at the table, with her laptop open, bifocal reading glasses on, halfway down her nose, and in a floral sundress. She was so frail looking. There were bagels in a basket on the table and place settings, iced glasses, a pitcher of lemonade, chilled vodka, and fresh flowers arranged perfectly. My mother's mess of mail, papers, and her bulky laptop was confined to her space.

"Rrro-Rrro, Mees Carrie ees here!" he announced loudly to my mother, cheerfully rolling those R's. She swirled around in her chair and looked over her bifocals, smiling. The first thing I noticed was the oxygen tube wound around her ears to her nose, the tubing led to a tank on wheels, right next to her. She had bloodwork cotton balls covered with band-aids on both arms. Her hair was a bit redder and greyer, she looked smaller, but her bright lipstick and make-up was perfect. She still wore a ton of bangle bracelets and had on ridiculously over-priced shoes on for someone her age.

She popped her glasses off, letting them fall on the chain, landing on her chest. Yep, no doubt about it, my mother had aged. No longer looking like Madonna; instead, she was slowly morphing into Bette Midler. "Oh, Carrie, you're here! I didn't think you'd actually come," she said, obviously lying, considering the set up that was laid out. She stood up, slowly and walked towards me a bit, tethered to her oxygen tank, giving me a big, unexpected hug. I was too surprised to hug back "Seet, seet, Mees Carrie," the camp Latino said, as he pulled out my chair. "Have a seat, Care. Tony has some lunch for us. What do you think, you like the house?" she asked, looking out the huge windows to the gorgeous in-ground pool, beyond to the waterway and the boat docked there. "Now you have a pool," I stated coolly, sitting down. My mother noticed my tone. "Tony, honey, give us a moment, will you?" The Spanish fly nodded and flitted out the double glass slider to the pool area. I leaned forward, agitated.

"Honestly, Mom? You have your own Agadore Spartacus house boy? I feel like I just walked into a scene from Birdcage and you're Nathan Lane! What is going on? Who is this guy? The pool boy? A caretaker? Are you sick? Is that why you called me here?" "Okay, slow down.

Jeez. You don't come by for years, and you want all the answers in a minute. Calm down, fix yourself a bagel. You want salmon? I got smoked salmon and whitefish salad in the fridge." "What the — what are you Jewish now?!" I couldn't help but shout, I was so surprised by her transition into this lifestyle, which was a world away from my upbringing.

"I'm blending in!" she shouted. And we were right back at it.

"Mom, you're a step away from becoming Lainie Kazan. What the hell is going on?"

"Can't we even have a nice meal together without getting straight into a fight? It's been ten years, Carrie."

"Who is that guy?"

"That's just Tony. He helps me around here." "Like... a boy toy?"

"Oh, good grief, Carrie. Really?!" she pounded the table with her fist for effect. "Look at me! Do I look like someone who needs a toy boy? I'm strapped to a friggin' oxygen tank here! He's my aide. He takes me back and forth to the doctor's. I have stage... whatever... I don't know, stage-fucking-30 ...lung cancer. So, he helps me."

She takes a few breaths. "He's my carer, support worker, whatever. I pay him to help me, okay? I can't do the things I used to do. Like take a shower, put on my fucking makeup, do my goddamn hair, get groceries, for Christ sake, alright? I get exhausted after 20 steps! Now can we have a nice lunch?!"

There was a long pause as she schmeared her bagel with cream cheese.

"I...okay. I didn't know. How would I know that?" Now, I sounded like the Jew. "I'm sorry, Mom. I...just didn't know." I said quietly. My mother shrugged a big Jewish shrug of the shoulders and sighed.

"That's why I'm telling you. You don't come around, you barely call, you're off doing your own thing, and that's fine, that's okay, that's the way it should be. I don't blame you, you should be doing that. But I thought you should know that I'm dying. I'm gonna goddamn die, Carrie. Now, eat a fucking bagel," she demanded, almost out of breath. She pushed the basket towards me.

"Dying? This...wow...it's that bad?" I take a bagel, so she doesn't yell again. "I mean, there is no such thing as a stage thirty, right? But ...you're dying, they actually said that, the doctors?"

"Whatever. It's bad. They've used the word terminal, okay? They tried. I did whatever they said. Chemo. I had to wear a goddam turban all of last year," she says as she sets her bagel down.

"Mom, I'm sorry. I...I don't know what to say. I never thought anything could take you down." Oddly, I feel like I should touch her hand or something, but she's on a tangent.

"You heard me, right? A turban."

"I'm sure you rocked it. You've always been...fashion forward."

"I know. I'm just sick of all these tubes wrapped everywhere and being poked like a pin cushion day after day. And the symptoms are getting worse now. I've done all I can but ...whatever. I made my peace with it. Shit happens. Luck runs out. I didn't ask you here to pity me, so, listen. We got things we have to talk about now, you and me. Stop looking at me with sad eyes, Carrie, I swear to God, I'll reach over there and poke those peepers out. We've got things to discuss, you and me." I nodded and tried not to have 'sad eyes'.

Jesus, Carrie, I said to myself. Pull yourself together.

Silence hung in the air like a thick fog for a moment. I could barely swallow the bit of bagel I had picked off and stuck in my mouth. I must have looked like it because my mother poured lemonade over a tall glass of ice and topped it off with plenty of vodka.

"Here," she said, sliding the glass towards me, "You probably need this."

"Jesus, Mom... Are you ...gonna ask me, to...to...?"

"What? Kill me? Like assisted suicide?" She laughs out loud.

"No! I mean, like... tell me...like... your... uh, last wishes?" I asked softly.

"Oh, please, Carrie! Don't get all tragic on me. I already have my cemetery plot chosen and paid for; my coffin is picked out, and everything is taken care of. I'm sick, I'm not an idiot. That shit is done and dusted."

"Okay...odd sense of morbid relief ...I don't even know what's happening right now," I say, taking another sip of my drink.

"Listen," she said, looking around to be sure Tony was still out on the patio and then leaning across the table, she continues, "The IRS and the FBI are going to seize this house, the cars, the boat, everything. I got a tip from a reliable source on the inside. It's going to happen. I knew it would. I haven't paid taxes for years..." she shrugged, "and…rightfully so. I dodged them for as long as I could. So, they're coming for all of it. Will I be dead or alive, who knows? It's in the process, so it'll be soon, I'm told. I've got a lawyer looking into it, but even he says the jig is up. "

"Jesus, Mom. But maybe-" she cut me off and leaned in closer.

"Now…here's the thing…" She stopped and looked out the doors to see Tony skimming the pool now, before she continued again in a lower tone, "I told Tony I was leaving everything to him." Her eyebrows popped up as she spoke, almost delighted. My eyes widened, "What? Why, why would you do that? Oh, my God, Mom, what is the matter with you?"

"Now, don't get mad, Carrie. I know. It's shady. I know it is. But, look, I pay him well, so don't feel bad. Thing is, I just don't want him to leave right now. I need someone here. I'm not stupid, I know by telling him that, it's what's keeping him here. So, I had to. If I told him the truth, he'd leave. And listen, I didn't forget about you. I got something for you. Come on, follow me."

GOOD AT IT

She grabbed the handle on her mobile oxygen tank wagon and rolled on through the house. It took me a good minute to close my mouth. That was a lot to process in a small amount of time. My mother was dying, and she was leaving everything, yet absolutely nothing to her gay, black, Latin, caretaker-pool boy-hustler-maid. I could only imagine what was in store for me.

I was numb to the point of not even knowing if my legs would work, but somehow, I followed my mother through the house, past a sun-lit, posh living room with more sliding glass doors overlooking the water and then down a hallway to her insane-looking, Paisley Park purple ostentatious bedroom. I look around the room. "Is that a...purple... flamingo statue?" She ignored me. I looked around. "Oh, Mom, come on. Even Prince would vomit in here." "It's calming!" she yelled.

"It's alarming, is what it is."

"In the closet, there's a Payless Shoes shoebox," she said, motioning for me to get it. "Just like the old days, huh?" I said, opening the closet door. She nodded. She sat in a large, high back white velour chair next to the bed. She sat up straight, proper like she was going to knight me any second. I looked back at her for a second and shook my head at her flair for the melodramatic before I bent down past her assortment of sundresses and saw the box she was talking about. When I was younger, my mother always told me there was a shoebox in the closet with "the ugliest pair of shoes you've ever seen," apparently, so I wouldn't forget them. That box had a fake bottom and under that were cash, passports, and a business card with a "guy to call" if she ever got picked up by the police.

Occasionally, as any teenager would, I'd swipe a twenty-dollar bill if I needed cash. Not too often because I was always worried she would count it and bust me. As sure as the sun was shining, there was the pair of horrible, ugly shoes in a Payless box. I handed it to her. She opened the lid, and beneath the bottom was cash, her passport and business cards. She slid her fingers around more and then took out a small key lying under it all and unlocked the top drawer to her nightstand.

"Put the key back in and put the box away." I did as she asked. She pointed to the bed. I sat down. She opened the drawer and took out a notebook, the only thing in it, and she rested it on her lap. "For you," she said, patting it. "What's that?" I asked. She opened the notebook. There were scribbles, writing, drawings, circles, arrows, sketches, numbers that I couldn't make out from where I was sitting... I had no clue.

"Schematics," my mother said. What the-? I was confused and subconsciously holding my breath.

"Carrie," she dropped her voice lower, looking towards the door, then back to me. "Carrie, these are the plans for what I wanted to be ...my last big score. The biggest. Bengal's of Bal Harbour." She waited for a second for my reaction, but then kept going when there wasn't one. "I want you to have them... It's fool-proof. You'd be set for life." Boom. There it was. And my whole body instantly deflated. "You want me to rob the largest jewelry store in Bal Harbour, Miami?" "Yes." "For you?" "No! For you! I'll be dead in a month." She stood up and held the notebook out to me like Rafiki holding Simba on the mountain top in 'The Lion King'. "I'm giving you the keys to your very own kingdom!"

"Oh, for fuck's sake!" I yelled, shoving the notebook out of my face. I was flabbergasted. I didn't even have the words to explain what was running through my mind.

She sat back down. "What? Look! I have the plans all figured out. Right here! Every detail is written out! All you need to do is read the notes and follow them to the dot. It's a beautiful, flawless plan, my best work," she said beaming. "Oh, Carrie, don't look at me like that. Come on. You can get out of that nightmare of a city. It's full of hoodlums, for god sakes, people are floating over on tires from Cuba and taking over!" "Jesus! Mom how racist can you be?" "I'm not racist! I employee a Latino right now! How am I racist?" "You are!" "Listen to me, this is a big score. If I had done this years ago, we'd be living large in Beverley Hills right now, without a care in the world." "That's YOUR dream, not mine."

"Carrie. Do this job. Then get out of here. Go someplace quiet, nice, with a fucking pool. Start your own restaurant, write a cookbook, work on your own terms. Or ...don't work at all! Enjoy life! That's all I ever wanted for you. To be sure you were happy and enjoy life." "I am happy! I have what I need!"

"But, is it what you want? There's a real difference."

"Look, Mom, this is your thing. It's how you live, not how I live. I don't want to always have to worry about going to jail. I don't want to be looking over my shoulder all the time. I want to settle down with a nice woman, live a decent life, and create world-class food. Is that so much to ask for?" "Carrie, serving up gourmet tacos for the farkakte Miami Sound Machine is just a JOB. You work sixty hours a week, on your feet, sweating over an open flame. You don't get to enjoy life. This is the perfect score. One night. Bam! Remember, you used to say that all the time? Bam! Like that Portuguese cook from New Orleans. What was his name? Emerald? DiGrassi?" "Emeril Le Grasse, mother." "Yeh, him! Bam! Honey, Carrie…there's over four million in jewels at Bengal's …right in the front cabinets alone! Even if that's all, you walk away with! Four million. If you get more, then Mazel to you. You fence them at the place I wrote down in this book, and you're set for life. It's all arranged. Jim is my fence. We've done business for twenty-five years. He knows his cut. I trust him. He knows you're coming, he's lining up buyers. You have nothing to worry to about. He's low key, he's successful, and he's been moving ice for years. Mazel to him." "Mazel? Listen! Yentel, it's not happening."

I stood up and turned towards the door. "Carrie, wait!" "What?" "You know why I named you Carrie, don't you?" "Yes, because Carrie Fisher was your idea of what every woman should be." She nodded. "Let's face it. You're no warrior princess, but you got moxy. kid. And you're smart."

"Sorry to disappoint you, Al Capone."

"You aren't a disappointment. Don't ever think that. I ...I wanted to do this myself and just give it all to you. If I could, I would. But I can't now. It's too late. I missed the window because I wanted my plan to be perfect, and that takes time. Also..." she paused. "I sure didn't plan on getting sick! Now, I feel bad that there's nothing but a few grand in a safe deposit box at Sun Bank for you when I die. It's not enough. It's peanuts. You deserve more. I put you through a lot as a kid. Things didn't work out in the end. I got greedy, I thought I could fuck the government, and now everything I wanted you to have is getting taken away. I'm not proud of it, but that's the truth. So, when I thought about, this is the better thing to leave you," she said as she patted the notebook.

"Well. That's quite a legacy, Norma Desmond."

"Oh, Carrie. Stop. You can do this. You got guts. You make me proud. Always have, with your fancy food, and big career. But this could change your life and make it even better and then

I'll be looking down on you satisfied that I did right."

I laughed a bit, "Oh, Mom, let's be honest. You'll be looking up, not down."

"Well, either way, I'll be amongst friends." She grinned. "I'm sure you'll all have VIP seating in The Winner's Circle of Hell."

"Alright, look, stop being a crap bag. It's so perfect, why do you have to doubt me? I've been doing this forever. Have I ever been caught? No. I'm good at this, and I always have been," she explained, ignoring my comments and returning to the business at hand, she continued. "Bengal's has their air conditioning units on top of their building, you can see the condenser fan up there. You can access their roof around back, there's a ladder on the wall, you pop a few canisters of sleepy gas in the unit, it pumps into the store, you take your time, the guard passes out, you put your gas mask on, go in, get your haul and you're out. You take your time, make no mistakes, and your home free. I know, I make it sound too easy, but you'll need to study the notes. Case it. See for yourself. I even got the gas canisters, KO in a can, and I got the masks, they're in the garage. Everything you need is in the box my Kitchen Aide mixer came in-"

"Stop telling me the plan, Mom! I'm not doing this."

"Oh, come on!" she yelled, smacking her notebook.

"You go find that Missy Mathers girl, she's your 'nice woman to settle down with' and you know it," she paused for effect, "You do this and make off with the goods like in that movie 'Bound', and you've got yourself a big muff diver happy ending!"

"This is not a Gina Gershon movie! By the way, It's Michelle, Mom, her name is Michelle …and are you fucking kidding me? Muff diver? Really? Is this a truck stop at Florida Georgia line?"

"What? You didn't know I knew that you were a lesbian? I don't care! Like I said, whatever makes you happy. Some people like steak, some people like clams, makes no difference to me. I got little Latin Liberace working for me, I'm fine with the gays."

"I mean, are you fucking kidding me about getting Michelle Matthews involved in this mess?"

"You two were made for each other all through your high school years, so why not ride off into the sunset together? In a brand, new

Maserati, no less! Am I right?" She really did seem absurdly delighted with this plan she had hatched up. I wondered if her pills made her goofy.

"Mom! Seriously!"

"She's still single, you know? Her parents sold that flower shop in the last year or so and moved to Phoenix. Phoenix. Who lives in Phoenix? Yuck. Like living in a beige blow dryer. I keep in touch with some of the old geezers in Margate. It's a shame, the shop is just sitting there empty. Vacant. The old delivery trucks still sitting in the parking lot. New owners haven't done anything with the place yet. Anyway, Michelle is in Fort Lauderdale, bartending at some place called Bootlegger's."

"What?"

"You heard me. Bartending. Bootlegger's." She stared at me, letting the statement that linger.

I paced nervously and began gnawing at my thumbnail. I hadn't thought about Michelle for a long time. My mother watched me waiting a minute. "Go rescue her, Carrie."

"Oh, stop it, Mom!" I would have been laughing if this wasn't my life. "Jesus, this isn't some 'Ocean's Eleven' movie you're directing here!" We both heard the sliding door open in the living room.

"Rrrro-Rrrro, are you ready for lunch? Eees Mees Carrie still here?" Tony was wandering down the hall. My mother shoved the book in her nightstand, slammed it shut and stood up, grabbing her oxygen wagon.

She stopped in front of me and shoved her finger in my face. "Just think about it."

"Stop it." I batted her hand away, lazily, but she held mine. "Don't say anything. Not a word. Just think on it." She let go of my hand and shuffled to the doorway. "I may have screwed up your childhood –"

"MAY have?"

"At least, let me die knowing I'm giving you the opportunity for a fucking amazing adulthood."

"Quit it," I said in a harsh whisper.

"Ooo…Here joo are," he said, standing in the doorway, "We have lunch and den you take your peels," he said, pointedly towards my mother.

"I'm not dead yet, you don't have to yell," my mother muttered, walking past him. Agadore Spartacus Jr. then led us back to the kitchen table where I choked down the bagel and slammed most of that vodka drink. After some small talk, my mother appeared tired and excused herself for a nap. I walked her to her room and helped her into bed, covering her up.

"I know you only want the best for me. I know it's what you've always wanted for me." I said to her, smoothing her blanket.

"I can't give you what I had planned to anymore, but I can give you the future you deserve. I know, wasn't the best mother, Carrie, and I've spent the last ten years regretting that. But I do love you with all my heart."

"I love you, too, despite all your Shirley MacLaine wackiness."

"Shut up, you. And close the door on your way out." Her eyes still had that sparkle like they did when I was younger. She gave me a cocky, self-assured smile as she closed her eyes. I did as she asked, closing the door and made my way back in the kitchen where Tony was cleaning up. I gathered my dish and glass and brought them to the sink, where he was washing a glass platter.

"Alright. What's your deal?" I asked nonchalantly. He sighed and turned off the water, spinning around to face me.

"Okay. Fine. You wanna play it that way? Fine," he said, in perfect English. "You waltz in here just as your mother is on her last dying leg, swoop in and think she's going to leave you everything because you've had a change of heart and re-connected? After you've been gone for years? While I've been the one right here, taking care of her. I'm sure it's driving you nuts, but she's made up her mind. She's leaving everything to me." I nodded, listening to him.

"Hey, Charo. Easy there. You're right. It's all yours. She told me I'm cool with that. What makes you think I want anything, anyway? I'm fine with what I have, with what I've worked for. I have everything I need."

I took the last swig of my drink and handed him my glass, folding my arms in front me, staring at him. I leaned on the counter. I knew there was more. I was right. He wasn't finished. "Oh! Okay, with your high and mighty attitude. Let's go down that road then. I'll make it simple. I'm here every day, I make your mother smile and laugh while she gets treatment after treatment, I was the one who sat next to her when she learned her diagnosis, I'm the one maintaining this place and making sure she takes her pills and isn't putting on two different shoes every day or lipstick on her eyebrows!"

"Oh well done, RuPaul. Just remember who endured the teen years with her. The endless phone calls day in and day out, while I was trying to study, go to school, and make something of myself."

Stepping away from the sink and smacking a dish towel on his leg, Tony makes an exaggerated hand on hip statement.

"Hiding away in Miami, making excuses not to visit, distancing yourself. What for? Because you're ashamed? You chose for it to be like this and I don't feel bad in the least that she's leaving me everything. I used to hear her calls to you. They lasted three minutes. You couldn't get off the phone fast enough."

"Whoa, man! Hold up. Do you think I don't know WHY you've done all this? Why you're watering her goddamn plants? Skimming leaves out her pool? Oh, I know why. Don't you dare pretend to care, pal. My mother is the pot of gold at the end of your gigantic, fucking rainbow." He clutched his heart as I finished speaking, like a dying amateur dramatics performer.

"Oh, and another thing, you don't know anything about our past, do you? Did she tell you about all the times she brought home the strange men she was hustling out of their life savings with her new and creative scams? Did she tell you about the times that she would bribe and blackmail my friend's fathers, my teachers, our city officials which ended up forcing us to move all over the country? No? She didn't tell you that? We moved three times a year, buddy. I have too many memories of packing up in the middle of the night and not knowing where we were going next. Did she tell you about her escapades with the four-foot tall horse racing jockeys just to get tips for who to bet on? Did she mention how she used me and my friends like day laborers? Or how she used to fight with my grandmother for the whole neighborhood to hear? How she emasculated my father so bad he just up and left? Don't tell me about MY childhood, Tony. Didn't you ever think there might be a reason why I wanted to stay away?"

"Yeh? Well. That was then. Right now, she treats me good, I treat her good. That's what I know. From where I'm standing, regardless of what your mother was doing, she never left you. You left her. She didn't leave you. That's more than I can say for my mother."

"Oh, boo-fucking-hoo, Nancy. You're using her. Look at you, in this big mansion, biding your time while you think you're playing my mother in a long con. You two are a perfect match. Have it all. I don't want any part of this."

"Good, because it's in her will! You can dispute it if you want, it's ironclad in writing, legal and binding! But most importantly, it's what she wants!" he hissed.

"You have nothing to worry about, you piece of shit," I said as I stomped to the door.

"Fuck you!" he yelled.

Chapter Five

I left after that heated exchange, and the long drive back to my condo in Miami, my mind was swirling in thoughts. He obviously suspected nothing about the Feds showing up to confiscate everything soon. I was livid that he dared to con a dying con woman, and yet it didn't surprise me. I flipped between being angry about it and being happy that my mother was smart enough to burn him at his own game. I spent every spare moment of the next few weeks sitting on my balcony, staring at the skyline, deep in thought about everything that went down that day. I struggled with where I was at in my life and where I wanted to be, and what it would take to make it better. Did it all come down to money? I wasn't struggling. I was okay. Wasn't I?

Before that day, I was perfectly okay with my life, my career, and my choices. After that day, I questioned everything. Did it secretly gnaw away at me that I was more like the father I never knew? Was that bad? Why was being a decent, honest person such a bad thing? Should a person be rewarded for that? Are they ever? I mean, an honest day's work warranted an honest day's pay, but is that it? A few crappy vacation days to visit Disney World, put yourself in debt, and work to pay it off before starting all over again? It didn't sound that great when I had put it that way.

Was I genetically pre-disposed to such shitty genes that I was seriously considering my mother's offer? And why now? What was it that I really wanted, as opposed to just having what I needed? Was my mother's way of thinking so bad? Would it be awful to ignore her last wish ...that I ultimately have what I want? It certainly helps with peace of mind. Well, not for her because she was always looking for the next big score. I wouldn't be like that. Would I? No, I could recognize the flaws in that mentality. Having enough IS enough for me. A couple million is definitely enough. But the question remained. What did I want? My own restaurant? Or just to not work at all and just cook for the sheer joy of cooking? But for who? There's no one in my life that I care enough about to share that with. Is it Michelle? It's Michelle. It's always been, Michelle. But so much time had passed. Would she feel the same way?

Day after day, all those things and more weighed heavily on my mind. I wasn't myself. I was sad about my mother's condition. I was sad that she was upset at herself for being too greedy in the end. I was sad that I had no one to talk to about all of it. I realized that I closed myself off to people, co-workers, lovers because I was profoundly scared of anyone knowing me or what my life was like because of my mother. The only people that knew the truth accepted it and kept my secrets were Bodega Bobby and Michelle. Good or bad, I could always be myself with them. Even if I did carry out my mother's plan and no one else knew but those guys, things would be okay. Finally, after a lot of sleepless nights, I had made my decision. I may have had my doubts about my mother's life advice, but I never doubted her "career". I was trusting in her now. I wanted her to be happy in her last days.

The only problem with that was my mother had died three days earlier. I felt awful that I didn't take her as seriously as I should have when she said, "I'll be dead in a month." I felt awful that I couldn't tell her I had made a decision and I would do as she wanted. I knew it would have made her happy. I stood on my balcony, looking out over the city, hoping she knew now. Hoping she would finally rest easy.

I sat quietly away from everyone at the cemetery. I recognized a few faces from Margate and the racetrack but had no connection with anyone. I was amazed by the fact that my mother, with all her flaws and her lousy choices, managed to always have a big circle of friends. The people that knew her loved her. She was always quick and sarcastic enough to make people laugh and never worried about who she offended or annoyed. She lived loudly and without grace, which both embarrassed me but impressed me. I knew my mother had no real sense of loyalty to anyone, not even my father. It was like she saved it all up for me. I never gave much of a thought to how I felt about her when I was busy in my everyday life. I didn't feel a void when I moved away. I guess because I always knew my mother was a phone call away, as selfish as that sounds. But sitting there, with the drone of the preacher and the birds chirping, I felt it. I felt the void.

After the typical formalities were over and everyone had left, I stayed. I sat under a big bushy tree a few feet from her plot, where I just watched her be lowered into. I cried for what felt like hours. Not entirely sure why or where it was all coming from. I took solace in that our last words were "I love you." Well, just before the "Shut up and close the door on your way out." I found comfort in my mother's, albeit twisted, way of looking out for me right until the very end. A fail-proof jewelry heist of my very own. I actually laughed out loud at the thought. But, it was what she knew. And she was good at it like she had said a long time ago. I remembered that conversation so clearly and how she lit up when she said, "I'm good at it, Carrie. I really am." So, I stood up, brushed off my jeans, and took a deep breath. "Let's hope I'm good at it, too, Mom."

From that moment, I set my sights on how to get my hands on that notebook now that she was gone. I had an idea, though, but I had to suck up my pride and hope my mother was right about Michelle.

I knew "Bootlegger's" bar well. It had been a hot spot back in the day, perched on Fort Lauderdale's intercostal waterway next to two other bars, "Shooter's" and "Dirty Nelly's," and it was THE place to be in the '90s. Reachable by car or water taxi, the three bars more or less ran into each other all overflowing with people, spilling onto the docks. It had the perfect Florida atmosphere, often hosting hot bod contests and pool parties. With more and more night clubs opening, though, and South Beach in Miami becoming a focal point for tourism and Spring Break, it had lost a bit of its appeal to that crowd, and was now a more calm, local, laid back marine lover's hang out. It still had that familiar feel to it, though. It was early, and not many people were there. I headed to the bar, where I laid eyes on Michelle, slicing lemons, chatting with a couple of boaters.

She looked over at me and went back to chatting before doing a double take. A slow smile spread across her face as she wiped her hands on a bar towel just to place them firmly on her hips, shaking her head, chuckling. "Well, well, well…"

"Hey, stranger," I said, sounding about as cliché as it comes. She ducked beneath the server's slot and popped out from behind the bar, landing in front of me.

"Carrie. It's so good to see you!" She hugged me tightly, and said into my ear, "I'm so sorry to hear about your Mom."

"Thanks, it all happened sort of fast," I said, "for me, I mean. We kind of grew apart for a while. I didn't know a lot of what was going on."

She nodded, understanding without me having to elaborate. She smelled like Australian Gold suntan lotion and looked amazing in her faded cut off shorts and white "Bootlegger's" polo. Her hair was pulled back in a ponytail, she had cool rope, leather and silver bracelets on and face showed little signs of aging.

"How're you doing with it all? It must be rough, I'm sure, but…seriously, you look really good," she said, pulling out a seat at an empty table, gesturing for me to sit. She sat opposite me to keep an eye on the bar.

"Thanks, I'm okay. Things are okay. It's all kind of surreal. Going through the motions, pretty much, I suppose. But what about you? Looking fantastic. Keeping the legend of Bootlegger's alive, I see?"

"Yeah, I guess. I mean, I don't love it, but it's fun. After art school, I just couldn't find a job. Imagine that? No one wanted to pay me to make art," she laughed, "so, I worked part-time waitressing and part-time in a craft store, teaching water-color painting classes a few nights a week. And somehow, it's just evolved into this." She threw up hands. "What can I say? I didn't hold up my end of the bargain," she grinned.

"What do you mean?"

"You said I'd be a famous artist and you'd be a famous chef."

"Maybe fame isn't all it's cracked up to be. Besides, my grandmother used to say, 'fly under the radar'. Maybe being anonymous is the way to go and I think we're doing that pretty well at that part." "Agreed," Michelle said, with a small chuckle. "So, um, are you-" I started. "Do you have-" Michelle began at the same time. We laughed for a second.

"Single," Michelle said, throwing up her hands.

"Same," I said. "Big surprise, right?"

"Wow, we are two total losers, aren't we?" Michelle laughed.

"Independent losers!" I said. Michelle reached across the table and touched my hand. "Carrie, I really am sorry about your Mom. She was a crazy, irreverent, spontaneous, fly by the seat of your pants kind of woman. Which, I know, was hard for you. But come on. You have to admit, she was fun," she said with a wink. I nodded my head with a small sideways smile, thinking, and looking at her slender, tanned hand touching mine. Michelle giggled at her thoughts.

"Do you remember the time we were on your patio talking about Debbie Battaglio's thirteenth birthday party and the spin-the-bottle game she had planned? We were all like 'Debbie said she's gonna give Doug Evans a hickey!'...and your mother overheard us from the kitchen window and came out to lecture us on boys and she told us..."

"Hickies cause cancer!" we both quoted my mother at the same time, laughing.

"Well, we figured out that was a lie when Doug Evans didn't die by our sophomore year," I said, shaking my head at my mother's ridiculous attempt at keeping us virgins.

"Or all the times she would tell us to go get in the car while she paid the bill for dinner at the diner," Michelle said, giggling.

"And she would just skip out without paying!" I finished the thought.

"But she always left a tip for the waitress!" Michelle recalled.

"Always."

"She always had the balls to go back, too, like it never happened! Just walk in a week later and sit down and order the Sunrise special!" Michelle dabbed her eyes with the back of her wrist. Thinking of all the funny stuff, laughing, now, perhaps I was finding that emotion.

"The funny part is, she always had the money to pay, she just liked the excitement of a dine and dash," I said, thinking about how she would throw her head back with a big laugh, as she sped away, clapping and high fiving me, the embarrassed, angsty teen.

"She was a character, Carrie. I'm gonna miss her."

"She drove me nuts, right to the end. But I'm gonna miss her, too."

After almost an hour of talk, the lunch crowd started trickling in.

"Listen, I'm on until four, and then I'm headed home." She did that thing where she tilted her head and bit her bottom lip a little. "Would you be interested in coming by? We could catch up more."

"Yeah. I would. In fact, I'll even make you dinner." She smiled and jotted down her address.

Later that night, after I had made us a spectacular poached salmon dinner, we sat on Michelle's patio, drinking wine. We had gossiped about everyone we had in common from the old days, talked about different relationships we had bombed at. Michelle casually had her legs over my lap, just like how we used to sit when we were out by her pool or on my back patio.

"Did you ever bring a girlfriend home to meet your Mom?" Michelle asked.

"Me? Oh, God, no. Well, maybe once. But I was so anxiety-riddled, knowing my mother would embarrass me, I couldn't relax. Seriously, from the moment she would say 'Ooo, Carrie, who's your, insert dramatic pause here, frrrriennnnd?' until the visit was over, I would be cringing. What about you?"

"Once. My senior year of art college, I brought home this girl who I had been dating for a few weeks. She was a total hippie chick. Dreadlocks, bare feet, hemp shirts, hairy pits, daisy tattoos, the whole nine yards," Michelle laughed, remembering, "...and my father grilled her so hard about her plans for the future and what kind of life she was setting herself up for, 'probably living under an overpass' I think, were the words he used, that she literally dumped me on my doorstep and left!"

We sat quietly for a minute or two, probably both thinking about back then. "Did you ever date any guys or did you always know you were gay?" Michelle asked.

"Martin Hanover," I said, taking a sip of wine, "it was a total bust. He was my assistant manager at my first Miami job in a café on Collins. We slept together once, it was so bad, and I had to do the 'it's not you, it's me' thing after that because if I had to look at his wang one more time, I would have vomited."

"Priceless," Michelle said.

"Keith Kennedy, freshman year of art school, awful. I just did it to be sure. And man, was I sure."

"What about in high school, did you have any girl crushes? You know, aside from me," I said, giving her leg a nudge with mine.

"Ha, ha. Um, I don't know what about you? Did you? Other than me?" She laughed.

We both thought back for a second.

"Holly Vanderkamp," we both said at the same time, then laughing, pointing at one another.

"That naturally blonde hair," Michelle said.

"The dimples!" I responded. She nodded with me, and we sighed a bit, probably both thinking about Holly and maybe other things too, for a minute.

"It's funny that my mother always knew but never pressed me about it." "Yeah, my Mom was definitely more accepting about it than my Dad.

I'd imagine your Mom would have been completely cool about it. After all, she loved her gays. Remember that one guy who used to do her hair? What was his name? He does a drag show in Wilton Manors now." "Phillip?"

"Yes! That's right! His drag name is Phyll Landerer! He does an amazing Phyllis Diller impression."

As the night air got cooler, we headed in to face the mess in the kitchen.

"I said I was good. I didn't say anything about being neat," I joked, as we stood looking at the kitchen.

"Don't worry about it," Michelle said, pouring us more wine.

"Mish, I hate that it took something as crappy as my mother dying to get me back here. I should have been a better- "

"Don't. Listen, I get it," she said, touching my arm gently, "You needed to create some distance from that part of your life, and I understood the reasons. I never thought anything bad about it. I knew why you had to go. But, honestly, I sure am glad you're back." All the sudden, it felt like we were back by the pool at her parent's house. Everything felt familiar.

She leaned towards me and kissed me, softly at first, then, more full-on, exactly how we used to kiss in high school. I felt myself getting so swept up in her all over again. My whole body responded as she pressed against me. It felt so good I had almost forgotten that I wanted to tell her about my last conversation with my mother. I slowly pulled back a bit to see her smiling face. I laughed a little. "What?' she giggled.

"This. Us. Again." I said, sort of blushing.

"Only without the van," she said, with a wink, her hands still on my hips.

"Um, right. Uh, about the van…." I started. She tilted her head like when a dog hears something weird.

From there, I led her to the sofa, sat her down, and brought the rest of the wine over to the coffee table for us. I proceeded to gently unfold the story of how my mother had a notebook with a plan that she had left for me with her last wishes and how it could potentially land me with a windfall of money or in a jail cell. I explained that I didn't want to give her any details at all because I didn't want to involve her in it to the point of being an accessory, but she cut me off.

"Fuck that. I'm in. I love you. I've always loved you. You know that, or you wouldn't be here right now. So...What do you need from me?" That was all I needed to hear. So true, so blunt, so simple. Just like that.

I was careful not to involve Michelle in the actual plan but explained that I had to get the notebook from my mother's house. She asked some questions, mostly about why I needed it but I held firm and didn't disclose anything, finally saying, "I just need it. I waited too long. I should have just taken it when she showed it to me, but I needed time to think. It had been so long since I had seen her."

"Okay, but what is it? Like...a treasure map or something?"

"Don't worry about it. I'm protecting you this way. What you don't know can't hurt you or in other words, implicate you," and as the words came out, I remembered my mother saying them to me.

She nodded. "Okay. I trust you."

We sat up into the early morning hours as I explained about Phoney Tony and the IRS. I told her about the shoe box, the Kitchen-Aid garage box, and the notebook I needed to get. I told her my idea of how to get them back in the gated community and my mother's house. She was all in, without asking any more questions. "Okay, so we need a few things to pull this off, don't we?"

"Yes."

We soon realized we needed a third man, and that we already had the ideal guy for the job - we needed Bodega Bobby. We also needed the old flower delivery van and actual flowers in order to get back in Boca De La Cruz, if the IRS hadn't seized everything yet. The biggest risk, I feared, was that we were running out of time or already too late. We had gone over the what if's, the how-to's and then we went over the scenario repeatedly. By the time we had it down pat, Michelle called Bobby to meet up. She thought it was best to keep the details even more minimal when it came to bringing him up to speed.

"He's shady as fuck nowadays, so that's good, in a way, but let's keep it about his task; the box in the garage and getting us home safe. Nothing else."

We met Bobby at a McDonald's parking lot in Coral Springs, near Margate. He chose the spot. I was so happy to see him, I jumped out of Michelle's car as she parked. He got out of his car, but he ducked back, and a second later, he reemerged with an adorable little girl wearing a little dress and a backpack, holding his hand.

"Oh, my God, Bobby!" I said, giving him a hug, "Who is this little angel?" Michelle joined us and gave Bobby a hug and kiss.

Bobby ruffled the little girl's hair, "This is my daughter, Carmen," he knelt next to her, "Can you say hi to your Aunt Michelle and your Aunt Carrie?" The little girl played shy and latched onto Bobby's leg, hiding behind him.

"Hi," we both said, fawning over how cute she was and how she looked just like Bobby.

"Come on, let's go inside. We have to get this little girl some breakfast before she goes to school, don't we?" he said, wriggling her off his leg. She gleefully hopped along, holding his hand.

"You guys look good. I'm glad you called. I missed my girls," he said, holding the door open for us.

We all got coffee and sat while Carmen ate her breakfast. Bobby was smiling away at us.

"Look at you two, together again," he said, sipping his coffee, grinning. It was crazy to think of Bobby as a dad. The last time I saw him, he was barely a man. Now, he was this giant, hairy, grown-up guy with muscles and tattoos. And a daughter.

GOOD AT IT

Michelle was enamored with Carmen, wiping her little face and laughing along with her.

"I gotta know, Bobby, who would ever have a child with you?" she joked. "Hey now, you broads left me high and dry, I had to find me a good woman," he sassed back, laughing. "I met Carmen's Momma about four years ago. Her name is Maria, and we fell in love, got married shortly after that and had this little peanut the following year."

"I cannot believe you're a Dad, let alone a husband," I said, "and...what about the...uh, business?"

"Still at it. It's no Scar Face empire, though. Gets a little rough and tumble now and then, but it's all good, all good. The bodega is still the bodega. My folks moved to Coral Springs a while ago, and Maria and I run the store now. I got the old house my parents lived in. Margate's still a shit hole. What can I tell ya?" he laughed. After a little more chit chat, mostly Bobby asking questions about Gloria Estefan, after I told him I worked at 'Bongo's', we got around to the part about my Mom passing away. Bobby was genuinely gutted to hear it and apologized profusely for not knowing. He dabbed his eyes with a napkin and said he wished he kept better tabs on her because he loved spending time with her. "She was a badass, Carrie. Like fucking Selma Hayek in 'Desperado' but before we even knew it was cool. She was an impressive lady. Making bank, however, she could."

"Daddy…" Carmen called Bobby out for swearing. He reached in his pocket for a quarter.

"You're right, baby. Here, go put this in the box for the Ronald McDonald House."

"It 'posed to go in the swear jar," she corrected him. "I know, but we don't have a swear jar here, and those kids need it more," he told her. She hopped down and proudly strutted over to put the quarter in the plastic box.

"So, Bobby, I think I might need some help getting a few things from mother's house," I said, cautiously approaching the topic.

"What do you mean?" he asked while keeping an eye on Carmen, who was trying to count the coins in the Plexiglas box.

"Before my mother died, she told me she had boxed up a few things for me in her garage. But, the thing is, she had this caregiver, who's kind of a …"

"Like a gay… bully," Michelle interjected.

"Well, fuck that. That shit is yours, girl!" he said to me, just as Carmen walked back up. She raised her little eyebrows and stuck her hand in his face. He automatically reached back into his pocket and gave her more coins which she spun around to happily take it to the charity box.

"I know, I know, Bobby. But, she left him the house, so I feel like he may give me a problem when I try to retrieve my box. So I want to make it less of a risk if you know what I mean."

"Wait a second, she left him her house? What the hell?"

"No, it's cool, Bob. The IRS and FBI are gonna take it all anyway," said Michelle.

"And he has no idea," I added.

Bobby nearly choked on his coffee and then busted out laughing so hard, he had to hold his stomach. "My God, that's hilarious! Oh man, I loved your mother! That's…literally priceless! See? Desperado, like I told ya. Total badass. Only your mother would pull something like that. I love it."

He checked his watch. "Okay, so what do you need from me? Rough him up? Scare him? Because I should get the baby peep to school in a few. What's the plan? A bat to the knees, a beat down?"

"No, no. We don't want anything bad to happen. Not at all. Michelle and I thought maybe it would be best to try and get into the gated community disguised by delivering flowers. In the old flower shop van. This way I can get in, get to the house and try to talk to Tony all civilized, like grown-ups. Nothing violent. No thug moves. I think I can reason with him over the dumb thing I need."

"Oh, snap! Okay. Good thinking! The old van! It's still there! Both are still around back! I mean, I don't know if we can get in them or if it'll start, it's been sitting there for over a year now. But I know a guy that can hotwire it."

Michelle leaned forward, "Bobby, remember the secret key?"

He thought for a second. "The key! Yes! You think it's still there?"

"Why wouldn't it be? It was hidden so perfectly," she said with a big smile.

"We have to try it ourselves before involving your guy, okay? I want to keep this as much on the DL as possible." I asked, nodding my head for his reassurance. He nodded okay. "I need to keep this…minimal."

"Yeah, we really don't want any trouble. If Mr. Liberace is there, we'll just have a little chat. I mean, who knows, maybe the IRS has been there already. But, we need to try at least and get the boxes. That's all. No commotion."

"Right. Okay. Alright. All this sounds good," he said, before reaching in his pocket for another coin. "Here, Carmen, go put this in the box because Daddy's gonna swear again." She jumped for joy and took off as Bobby leaned across to us, smiling.

"Okay, ladies. Let's fucking do this."

We agreed that Bobby would drop his daughter off at school and meet us in the back lot of the bodega plaza in a half hour. We would check the delivery van for the key and then let him know if he needed to call his hot wire guy. Michelle and I watched him leave the McDonald's before heading off.

"He makes me a nervous wreck STILL, after all this time," Michelle said, as we drove down State Road 7.

"I know, he's such a thug now. Did you see the gun in the back of his pants when he leaned in the car to put the kid in the safety seat?" I asked.

"What? No! Oh, god. We have got to tell him absolutely no guns. Shit, Carrie, are we making a mistake with him? I mean, he's a good guy, right? He's a Dad, for Christ sake. He's not going to do anything stupid, is he?"

"I don't think we have to worry. We made it clear. No trouble." After stopping to get a shit load of flower bouquets from a corner drug store and a cheap vase, Michelle and I made our way to the plaza and pulled around back. We parked the car and got out just as Bobby pulled around. He hopped out of his car, chirped the alarm and met up with us by the vans.

"Is it there?" He asked. "We haven't checked yet," I said. "Hey, Bob?"

"Yeah?"

I paused for a minute. "We need to do this without any guns, okay?" He lifted his shirt and turned around so I could see he had nothing on him. He nodded towards his car. "It's in the glove box. No worries, Care." He slung his big, heavy arm around my shoulders and we watched as Michelle looked at the dusty, worn out vans. She pointed at the faded number two on the back door and patted it for luck. "Come on, baby. Be there," she whispered. I keep remembering what my mother always told me about making sure there are absolutely 'no witnesses' when about to undertake unlawful activity. Thankfully, it was too early for anything in the plaza to be open yet. It was only just nine a.m., but I was keeping an eye out. "Here we go," she said, getting down low by the wheel well and reaching under, carefully running her fingers around. After a few attempts, I was starting to get worried. I didn't want to involve anybody else in this, even if it was Bobby's hot wire guy. I was biting my thumbnail, as usual.

"No fucking way!" Michelle said, as she stood up and presented me with the little box.

"Get the hell out of here! It's there!" Bobby exclaimed.

I opened the small, dirty, rusty magnetic box, and there was the key. I held it up for them to see. It was odd to see an actual key, instead of a big black fob, these days.

"Holy shit," Bobby said, laughing. "It's like a fucking ancient artifact or some shit like that!"

"Alright, let's see if she starts," Michelle said, taking the key and unlocking the door. Bobby and I stayed by the hood. The door creaked loudly.

"Ew, gross," Michelle squawked, getting into the stinky old van. She rolled down the window for air, making a face. She stuck the key in the ignition. "Well, good news, there's a half a tank of gas in it," she said, looking at the dashboard. She turned the key. Rrrr...rrrr...rrr. It almost started.

"Pump the gas first, then try again," Bobby instructed. Michelle tried again. It cranked a bit more but died again. "Okay, try again, pump it twice and give it a go. Last time, though, so we don't flood the engine." I could feel myself sweating in the bright morning sun. Bobby was beading up, too.

"Please, please, please," Michelle pleaded as she turned the key a third time. The engine roared, and dust blew out from the hood, but it was running. She opened the door and scooted over to let me in the driver's seat. "Yes!"

"Rev her up a little," Bobby said, "blow the crap out, juice her up a little," as he went around back, looking at the tires and exhaust to be sure everything was okay. I did as he told me. He was still shaking his head in disbelief. "This fucking thing," he said, patting the panel, chuckling to himself.

"I'll get the flowers!" Michelle said. She grabbed the bunches of flowers and vase and got in the passenger side. I made my way to the back of the van, stepping over a blanket and plastic buckets and unlocked the rear doors for Bobby, as Michelle began stuffing and arranging flowers into the vase.

Bobby hopped in. He flipped over an empty, old five-gallon bucket and sat up behind us, leaning between the two seats, just like the old days. "Seriously, you guys. Look at us. Like nothing's changed!" he said, shaking his head with a smug grin.

As Michelle arranged and fussed with the flowers and the vase, Bobby tucked a rolling paper in them to look like a note. I froze up in thought with a glance at the two of them.

It was almost like my mother knew. It was just like she had said. I was spinning out in my head, reliving our last conversation. None of us were living out our dreams, not even close to being on target for them.

Bobby was right. Nothing had changed. He was selling drugs in shitty Margate, okay with a wife and baby in tow now, but still working at that same old bodega. Michelle was bartending, not doing what she loved, painting. Me, working long hours for someone else, away from my friends, or any kind of life outside work. I hadn't been with "my people" in a long time, and Mom knew it. She also knew I was happiest when I was with them. She had "a plan," but it was much more than just robbing a jewelry store. She had brought us all together again.

"You guys, I have to make a quick stop before we get to the house, okay?" I asked.

"Sure," Michelle said. Bobby nodded.

We chatted away like no time had passed. It was Bobby that noticed that the old radio. I tried turning it on, but it didn't work. Neither did the air conditioning, which was a bitch. "Hey, we're lucky this thing even started," Michelle said. "I mean, my Dad took care of these trucks like they were his babies, but the people who bought the business, I don't think they've even touched them."

"I never even saw those people, not once," Bobby stated, "I heard they wanted to open a Korean barbeque restaurant, but they ran out of money."

"My parents wanted out so bad, they didn't even care."

"My Mom told me she had still kept in touch with some of the folks from the neighborhood," I said.

"Eew, remember old Mr. Markowitz? With those ugly feet, always in the flip flops?" Bobby said.

Michelle and I both cringed. "He had the hots for you, Bob," Michelle stated.

"Fucking pedo. Always asking me to clean his pool. So insulting!" Bobby exclaimed.

"No one needs their pool cleaned three times a week," I pointed out.

"Okay, he probably was a pedo, but I sure made some green off him. We always had gas money, didn't we?!"

We both nodded. "True." I pulled into the Sun Bank parking lot. "Okay. Keep the motor running, this won't take long."

"Whoa! Carrie! Are we robbing a fucking bank?" Bobby asked with wide eyes. Even Michelle looked like she was going to shit her pants.

"Oh, my god, you guys! No! I just need to get something. Wait here."

After the usual formalities, a bank manager escorted me into the vault to open the safe deposit box my mother had in my name. He stepped back while I unlocked the box. There were two things in it. A large manila envelope and a little pink golf ball. I picked up the golf ball. It was the one from our "super day of fun". She had kept it all those years. I held it to my chest for a second and blinked back tears. I reached in for the envelope and opened it. Four banded bundles of cash fell out. They were stamped "$25,000". I put it all back in the envelope. "A few thousand", my mother had said, like it was nothing. There was a hundred grand here.

The bank manager cleared his throat. "I can have that re-counted for you if you'd like, Ms. Thompson?"

I closed the lid to the box. "It's not necessary. Thank you." He stepped forward with a form. "I'll need you to sign here and here," he pointed, as he retrieved a pen from his inside jacket pocket. I scribbled an illegible scroll on the lines and tightened my grip on the envelope and the golf ball.

"Is that all, you'll close out everything?" I asked him.

"Indeed, it is," he stated, "and again, I'm very sorry for your loss. We'll close the account for you and forward any remaining confirmation paperwork to the address you've provided." I thanked him, and he escorted me all the way to the front of the bank, where a security guard opened the door to see me out.

I hurried across the parking lot and got into the van.

"You okay?" Michelle asked.

"Yep. Can you put this stuff in your bag?" I handed her the envelope and the golf ball I was clutching.

"What's this? Hey! Is this an old putt-putt golf ball?" she asked, inspecting the ball and showing it to Bobby.

"Yeah. Apparently, my mother had just as much of a good time as we did on our super fun day." Michelle looked at me and instantly knew what it meant to me. She held up the ball for a minute. Bobby nodded his head.

"Best day ever."

"That's really sweet," Michelle said, touching my arm.

We rode along kind of quietly, each of us thinking about that day probably a lot more than we ever had. It was like a silent bond for us back then and maybe more so in the current moment.

As I reached the security gate at my mother's residential community, I fully expected to see the old man guard who had greeted me last month. Instead, a large black guy in a uniform with a ball cap on stepped outside of the guardhouse to my window. I rolled the window down and let Michelle lean over and do the talking. After all, this was her specialty.

"Hi there," she said, cheerfully, "We're delivering flowers to the Roseanne Thompson estate, at 1151. We're sorry for the delay. There was a mix up at the cemetery."

He narrowed his eyes and peered in at the flowers Michelle held. His arms had tattoos, he was a bit of a baller-looking type, like maybe he was in a gang at one time.

"Wait here." He stepped back in the guard house and picked up the phone. After a minute, he stepped back out. "No answer. You can either leave 'em here or come ba–"

Michelle stopped him. "Is there any way we can just leave them with one of her staff, or on the porch? My boss is already so upset over the mix-up, I really don't want to make things worse for us, or the family. We'll be super-fast."

"I can't letchoo do that." He had a terrifying, baritone boom.

Bobby leaned between us and faced the guard. "Hey, bro. Could you let us in for a half pack of reds to party with and a twenty?" He flipped the top back on a pack of Marlboro reds which had a small vial of coke and a twenty-dollar bill tucked in it. He tilted it enough for the guard to see. I held my breath and stared straight ahead as the man leaned in to get a better look. He noticed Bobby's tats, too. A smile spread across his face. "Oh, shit, my man. Nice. Make your way in, peeps," he said as he took it and fist bumped Bobby. He tucked the Marlboro pack in his breast pocket, reached in, pressed a button, and waved us in as the wrought iron gates opened.

I didn't take a breath until we made the first right. None of us did.

"Jeeesus!" I squealed as we headed around the bend.

"Oh, my God, Bobby! That was insane!"

"Always prepared. Plus, I saw his tats. That old crew loved to party."

"It's like some secret language or something," said Michelle, looking at me. "Bodega Bobby got game!" she laughed.

Bobby agreed. "Still!"

We pulled up to the house. I parked next to the Mercedes. I turned to both Bobby and Michelle. "Doesn't look like the IRS has been here yet, expensive car in the driveway," Michelle stated.

"Okay, guys. This is it."

Bobby whistled, staring out the windshield at the house and car. "Oh, dios mio!"

"Bobby, listen, Michelle and I will go up the door and scope out the situation. If we get in, I'll figure out a way to open the garage door. Once it's opened, I need you to get the Kitchen Aide box and put it in the van. Keep the motor running, because I will fucking freak if this van won't start back up and we're stuck here. Got it? One box. Kitchen Aide. In the van. Keep it running."

"Got it. Go. I'll get up front and be the eyes." He said, shifting off the bucket.

Michelle and I got out of the van, as Bobby moved up to the front driver seat to keep his eyes on the garage door. Michelle and I walked up to the door. She still had the flowers. I rang the doorbell. Nothing. I rang the bell again and tried peering over the frosted glass decal window panels and into the house.

"I don't see anyone," I said.

"Should we try the door?" Michelle asked.

I reached for the doorknob and turned it. The door opened. We both looked back at Bobby. He gave us the thumbs up sign and kept looking around. I tentatively stepped inside, Michelle followed me. We stood in the foyer, looking around. There were flowers everywhere, stacks of mail. It was way messier than the last time I was there, but everything remained basically the same. Michelle set the vase down with the others.

"Tony?" I called out. Nothing. No response.

"Tony?" I yelled louder. We waited. Nothing again. "Hey, Lolita!"

"Paging, Mr. Twat Waffle?" I called out.

"Anyone?" Michelle yelled. We waited again. Nothing.

"Well, the IRS definitely hasn't been here yet," I noted, looking around at the furnishings.

I took a few steps towards the kitchen. Michelle went the other way, then stopped. A second later, she hurried into the kitchen.

"Carrie! Is that him? Out there, on the boat at the dock?" she said, pointing out back to the water.

We peered out the glass slider door to spot Tony and another guy sitting on the boat, a bucket of champagne on ice, shirtless with their trendy swimming trunks and sunglasses on, soaking up rays without a care in the world.

'Ugh, yep. That's him in the orange trunks. That mother fucker, living it up."

"Ew. Rico Sauve, much? Jesus. Well, get your rays now, Creep, because it won't be long before you have nothing." Michelle said, looking out there.

"Okay, I'll open the garage door and go get the notebook. You keep an eye on him and yell if he starts walking back up to the house." I opened a pantry door and closet before finding the door that led to the garage. I pressed the button on the wall, and the garage door slowly opened. Bobby hopped out of the truck. I pointed to the Kitchen Aide box, he nodded and grabbed it, as he took it out to the van, I pressed the button again to closed the garage door.

"Still out there," Michelle reported as I hurried past her and headed to the Paisley Park bedroom.

I rushed to the closet and grabbed the Payless Shoes box with the ugly shoes, dumped them on the bed, peeled up the bottom, and quickly found the key. I opened the drawer and snatched the notebook shoving it down the back of my pants. I closed the drawer, shoved the shoes back in the box, not even putting the lid on, tucked it under my arm, and headed out the room.

"Carrie! He's walking back up! Come on! They're coming back! We have to get out of here!" Michelle met me at the foyer.

"Did you get it?"

"Yes! Let's go!"

"What is that?" she asked, opening the door.

"Ugly shoes. I'll explain later."

"Oh, those are hideous!"

"Come on!" I said, a foot away from the front door.

"Hold it, right there!" Tony yelled. We both stopped.

"Fuck," Michelle whispered.

We slowly turned around to face him.

"What do you think you're doing? I told you before, your mother left ME this house and everything in it!" He said, walking closer.

Michelle stiffened at his tone. I took a different approach. I dropped my shoulders and sighed loudly, almost as dramatic as my mother would have done it.

"Okay, okay. Fine. You caught me. Yes, I came back because I wanted these shoes." I tilted the box towards him so he could get a good look at the shoes. He literally recoiled from them, as if I stuck a lit torch in his face.

"Ew, Oh! Yuck. Stop it," he said like I was holding Kryptonite up to Superman's nose.

"She could have taken anything, the door was unlocked, while you were out there tanning your nuts, you idiot," Michelle added.

"Fuck you, who are you, anyway?"

"Look, Tony," I said, trying a different, more gentle approach, "I'm not here to dispute anything. You were right, I don't deserve it. My mother and I led very different lives, and although I regret it, I can admit it. I only came here for the shoes." I held up them up again, and he cringed like they were a bag of dog poo.

"She bought them for my grandmother, but my grandmother passed away before she could give them to her and she couldn't bring herself to get rid of them. I just wanted to have them so I could remember them both," I said, doing my best to drum up some emotion.

"Alright, fine! Fine! Take the gaudy, stupid shoes and get out of here before I call the cops and report you for trespassing!"

Before he could say another word, Michelle and I hurried out, slamming the door behind us and ran to the van. Bobby threw it in reverse as we climbed in and we headed off.

"We good?" He asked, heading down the street.

"All good!" I said.

"You were amazing, Carrie!" Michelle said, squeezing my shoulders as we caught our breath.

"That jerk was in there? In the house?" Bobby asked.

"Yeah! But Carrie turned it into some kind of soap opera moment, and sweet talked him so we could get the hell out of there-"

"Whoa, check it out! It looks like the Feds or something!" Bobby said, slowing down a bit as we all looked at the dark tinted windows and government plates on a bunch of big black SUV's passing us. "Holy fuck, the hairs on my neck are standing up!"

"Wait, wait, slow down, let's be sure," I said, cranking my neck around as far as I could to see.

"Ok, hold on, if I round the bend, and pull over, we can all see out the back windows and still be out of sight," Bobby said.

He did exactly that, and we all crammed our faces in the dirty back door windows, watching five men in dark windbreakers and three men in suits exit the parked SUVs all over the driveway and lawn of my mother's house. They banged on the door. A second later, Tony appeared, there was an exchange of words before one of the men shoved a bunch of papers in Tony's face and pushed past him. Tony was livid, going by his body language: stomping his feet and shaking his head, yelling, and following them in. I reveled in the moment. Bobby and Michelle had matching grins.

"Good job, Mrs. T.," Bobby whispered to himself, looking up to the sky.

"The look on his face! Ok, we need to get out of here, but that was totally worth it," Michelle said, elbowing me.

"She's right. That's enough. Let's go," I said, wanting to get out the neighborhood entirely at this point. As Bobby drove through the open gates, the security guard gave us a nod.

"Oh, my God, oh my god," Michelle murmured to herself, looking back to the gates, "We did it. We made it by the skin of our teeth," still squeezing my arm.

"Jesus Christ, one more minute, and the whole thing would have gone bust!" I said. I was sweating, my heart was pounding. Michelle was slowly exhaling to calm herself down.

Once, safely on the main road, after a brief bit of quiet, Bobby began to sing, "Growing up, you don't see the writing on the wall..."

"Passing by, moving straight ahead, you know it all..." I sang.

"But maybe sometime if you feel the pain, you'll find you're all alone and everything has changed..." Michelle sang. We all sang.

"I can see a new horizon, underneath the blazing sky, I'll be where the eagle's flying higher and higher, gonna be your man in motion, all I needs a pair of wheels, take me where the future's lying, St. Elmo's Fire," we sang together, "I can climb the highest mountain, cross the wildest sea, I can feel St. Elmo's Fire burning in me…" We had to. After all, it was the theme to our "super fun day" and somehow, it felt like my mother was with us. My eyes kept welling up. I held Michelle's hand, giving her a smile. It felt weird to me to feel this close to my mother now that she was gone. But I liked it.

We made it back to the plaza just after midday and Bobby put the box in the trunk of Michelle's car, being sure to keep an eye out for passers-by. Michelle locked the van up.

"I'm keeping this key forever," Michelle laughed. Bobby nodded in agreement, "Good deal!"

"Listen man. You were such a big help. Thank you," I said, giving him a big hug. Michelle hugged him, too. "Go be a Dad, big guy."

"This was fun. Nothing like a rush to start the day. I'm glad it all worked out."

"You're a good guy, Bob," Michelle said, punching him in the arm.

"Okay, ladies, it's been a pleasure. I gotta go run my store. Call me if you need anything more. Love you, dorks."

"Oh, we will. Love you, Cheech," I said, before heading with Michelle back to her car.

GOOD AT IT

Our parting words to Bobby weighed on my mind. "Go be a Dad,' and "Love you." I thought carefully about those words. I decided I couldn't involve Bobby anymore. The simple fact was that my mother always worked alone. Sure, she had her "people", her primary fence Jim and whoever's number she had written down to call if she ever got caught. But the thing is, she never got caught. She was never a suspect or a person of interest. She may have been the target of rumors here and there, but she never left behind any proof that would hold up in a court of law. All the years she had been scamming, robbing, stealing, and shoplifting, she never had a partner or anything. She never owned a gun, either. I was sure of that, and I had to do this her way. I had to do this alone. Bobby was a Dad now, and Michelle was truly the love of my life. I couldn't risk having them involved it what came next.

Chapter Six

I studied that notebook like it was a life or death SAT test, and I needed a perfect score. Any spare time I could manage, I cased Bengal's jewelry store. My mother's notes were accurate. There was a guard on duty in the store overnight. There was an air conditioning fan and condenser unit on the top of the building, and there was a fixed ladder leading up to it on the wall around the back of the building. She noted the type of alarm system and exactly what wires needed to be clipped on the panel box to gain entry to the back door, she noted camera points from the front and rear of the plaza. She had detailed lists of what was needed down to the wire cutters, the gloves, hats, and bags, to the gas mask. She also had mapped out the escape route and the exact point under the highway overpass where the notebook, clothing, and mask could be burned, leaving behind nothing. She had extensive research and dated pages of her dry runs with amendments and details. There were special notes written to me. "You can do this!" and "Relax."

I told Michelle that we needed to keep things normal: continue to work at our jobs, keep our regular schedules, and our residences and I would let her know the next steps. She wanted so badly to know the plan, but I convinced her that the less she knew, the better off she was. I told her that there was nothing to worry about.

We still did dinners, date nights, and sleepovers over the next month. I wanted my nerves to settle and to gauge any fall out from my mother's death. I needed to be sure the IRS or any government official, for that matter, wasn't going to show up at my door. We kept in contact with Bobby, met him for coffee, and finally met Maria. Things were back to usual. Nobody, not even my closest friends, would ever suspect, amid it all, I was going to rob the biggest jewelry store in South Miami.

Once I had decided on the date, I studied that notebook and did my research like my life depended on it, because it basically did. I was meticulous about the upcoming night, I had even checked the weather reports.

GOOD AT IT

It was gloomy and overcast all day, making that evening misty and creepy and perfect. I followed the plan to a tee. It was after 2 a.m. I parked away from the plaza, in an unsecured condo parking lot, where my mother had specified, mixing in with a big lot full of vehicles, made my way through bushes surrounding the lot and used the alley around Neiman Marcus to the back of the shops. Being mindful of the noted security cameras, I slowly made my way to the back of the plaza, undetected. Everything was going fine. It all matched everything in the notebook.

I had been there before in the day time, I knew the area well by now. All was going according to the plan until it came time for the climbing up the ladder to dispense the gas into the condenser unit on the roof. My fear of heights kicked in, but also there was also no way to avoid a specific security cam facing the ladder that wasn't noted in the book. It looked new. Maybe because of the work that was being done next door to the jewelry store, they had an extra camera installed. I couldn't use the ladder. There was no way to get to the ladder.

I stood frozen. It caused a wave of panic in me like nothing I had ever felt. I ducked behind a trash can and pulled out the notebook, scanning the pages to review the schematics of the store. I had to think on my feet. There was no plan B. I flipped through the pages, breathing heavily. "No, no, no," I murmured. I crept around the trash can and stared at the back door, thinking. I would have to cut the wires on the alarm panel on the back door, get inside, and unleash the can of gas inside the store by the main showroom, drawing the guard to the can of gas. It was risky. He would have time to radio in for back up. I thought, "Fuck, fuck, fuck!" over and over in my head. The whole plan was based on the guard passing out FIRST and then me entering the store, ensuring he would never catch a glimpse of me.

I had to push on. I had come this far. I looked at the schematics again to see the back room, where I would end up once getting inside. I hadn't focused on this part because originally, I wouldn't even need to know the layout of it.

My hands were shaking as I pulled the gloves on. I snuck back around the side of the building to where I could see the Bengal's front window, I watched the guard for what seemed like ages to get an idea of his rhythm, and pattern as he made his rounds. I crept around back again, staying close to the walls and staying low, dodging behind dumpsters and crates as I moved to the back door again and crouched down retrieving the small wire cutters out of my backpack. I had to pry off the front panel to get to the wires. I wiped the sweat from my brow and forced the panel door off and had to pry the face plate off, exposing the wires. Green, then yellow, fast snips, listen for the channel in the door lock to click. Once the wires were cut, the lights on the alarm panel went out, and emergency flood lights inside the store would come on. The door was unlocked now. I crept in. The back room was lit partially by the emergency lights. I reached for the thermostat on the wall and turned the air conditioning off. I didn't need the vents blowing the gas around now with this change of plans. If my count was correct, the guard was at the front of the store when the emergency lights came on, signaling a problem and he'd be making his way towards either the front, second alarm panel by the main doors or to the back.

I quickly took in the layout of the room. I saw the file cabinet I needed to get back to and duck behind once I opened the gas can. Close to the back door if I need to dash out. I quickly made my way to main showroom's entryway, peeked out as the guard was looking at the front alarm panel, pushing buttons. I pulled the pin on the can of gas and rolled it out, quickly, as the mist unleashed.

I could hear the guard's footsteps as he made his way to investigate the hissing sound from the can which was spewing out a cloud, not knowing what it was. I could hear him grappling with the can, grunting, coughing, and more clearly, his company radio, the static, and voices. He was calling it in, as I suspected he would. He struggled with the words "Base," he choked out. I could hear the company responding, "Omega 9 this is base, go ahead," Static again. "HQ base to Omega 9, come in? Omega 9, do you copy? We've received a distress signal from the alarm system. Sending patrol police now. Omega 9? Copy? Omega 9, status?" the sound was fading with the whizzing of the gas.

I quickly put my mask on and waited a second, until I heard the thud of his body hit the ground, out cold. Once he was out, I knew I had only a matter of minutes before the dispatched police arrived. I swiftly made my way to the front of the store, staying as low as possible as the mist of the gas rose upward and I found the drawer where the glass cabinets keys were kept, just as it was noted in the book. I cleared out every single glass case of its jewels and watches, methodically, from the front all the way to the back, stuffing them into the backpack in record time. The gas was thick and yellowish, I stayed focus even when I couldn't see right in front of me, I had the layout stamped on my brain. The smell of latex from the mask was making my stomach churn. I was already to the back door before hearing sirens in the distance. "You can do this," and "Relax" shot to my brain and played on a loop. I had known it was a possibility that the guard would signal to base before passing out, so the sirens were no surprise, but it did give me a jolt. My mother had noted that the average response time for Miami police was 4-7 minutes. My heart was pounding in my ears. As I reached the back door and crept outside, I pulled my mask off and gasped and gulped the fresh air.

I wanted so badly to be done with this, but I had to make my way back to the car. My knees were shaking as I stuffed the mask in the backpack while on the move. The bag was heavy as I slipped it around my shoulders. I just I had to keep my cool and keep an eye out for cameras, no getting sloppy now. I made my way down the alley, back through the bushes and to the residential parking lot where my car was. I crouched near a dumpster, out of the way from any lights, to cram my black hoodie, gloves, hat, and mask into my backpack before taking my ponytail out, transforming me from cat burglar to normal girl on her way to a night shift job. I began driving towards the area below the overpass, careful not to speed, which was my instinct, to just hightail it because the roads were quiet, being this late. The sirens faded the further I got from the scene. After driving to the particular spot that was carefully noted, I quickly pulled over where the homeless slept hard in their drunken hazes burrowed under cardboard and dirty blankets. I turned the headlights off and coasted just a bit in neutral before turning the engine off. Not one body stirred. I waited a moment just in case. I slowly and quietly opened my car door and crept to low-glowing can. I successfully dumped the evidence, as instructed, into the rusty tin drum that still had a low fire going from the usual hobo hand-warming gathering. The notebook, my hoodie, hat, hair tie, my gloves, the mask all going up in flames. I even tossed the wire cutters in, cautiously on top of my hoodie so it wouldn't make a noise.

All that was left in the bag was the jewelry and one torn page with Jim's phone number. I was finally on my way home. I could hear my heart beating and pulsing in my eardrums. I was covered in sweat and blasted the air conditioning right into my face. I didn't touch the radio. My thoughts were loud enough.

Once safely inside my condo, I dropped the weighty backpack on the floor next to the couch and plunked down with a deep sigh. My stomach was in knots, and my legs felt wobbly. It was 4:26 a.m. and I had done it. My adrenaline had yet to settle. I opened a bottle of wine and replayed the whole thing in my head a few times to assure myself I hadn't made any mistakes, even with the revised hiccup. I peeked in the backpack and looked at the goods, astonished at the load that was sparkling back at me. I didn't touch them or sort through them. I zipped the bag back up and pushed it under the coffee table with my foot. I drank, watched the earliest newscasts and waited to hear the magic words: "police have no suspects at this moment." As I sat there, flipping channels, back and forth to see every local news broadcast, I remembered how my mother did exactly this same thing. Only now I know what was going through her mind. There was only one breaking news report about police activity in Miami, reports trickling but no official statements and nothing further.

GOOD AT IT

Later, I woke up with the TV remote control still in my hand. The noon news was on, and there it was. A report of the Bengal's robbery, calling it a "multi-million-dollar jewelry heist". My jaw tightened just like my mother's used to, as I sat forward. "Miami-Dade police have no suspects at this time as they continue to investigate and ask for your help..." and they gave a public crime stopper tip line phone number. I sat back and blew out a hell of a sigh, running my fingers through my hair. No suspects. That translated to no leads, which meant no mistakes.

Over the next few days, I met with Jim and cut the deal my mother had lined up. We met at the Denny's diner, where my mother had brought me so many time as a kid. Jim looked like a department store sales clerk. He wore khaki pants and a blue polo shirt. He had neat, salt and pepper colored hair wore wire-rimmed glasses and had loafer shoes on.

I walked directly to him, and he stood up and hugged me quickly before sitting back down. "Good to see you," he said. I slid into the booth and dropped my backpack on the floor under the table like he specified in our initial phone conversation. He ordered us coffee from the waitress and made small talk. Mainly about what a character my mother was. I knew the plan was to have a decent length chat to ward off any suspicion. It was crowded, as usual. I wondered how many times Jim was in here and I just never noticed him because he was bland, normal looking and basically blended right in with everyone. I guess I always remembered that big, gross biker from the warehouse and thought everyone my mother did business with looked like him.

After about a half hour, Jim pulled out a five-dollar bill from his pocket and put it on the table as a tip. "I guess we should be off?" he said. I nodded. He reached under the table and grabbed the bag. He slung it over his shoulder and calmly walked up to the cashier and paid our bill. He turned and gave me a quick hug, said he'd be in touch and briskly walked to his car. It was the most of normal of things. I made my way to my car and drove home. The next day, Jim called.

Even with Jim taking his agreed share, I would still walk away with 5 and a half million dollars. We broke the transactions up over three visits to three different diners and cafes, always in a booth, always with the same bag swap procedure. The European buyer was happy with the score, Jim assured me, and we parted ways at the final meeting. I had my final gym bag full of cash. My "business" was done. I was relieved and astounded how Jim handled everything. It all went so smoothly. I thanked him again. "You're good at it, kid," Jim said, with a pat on my shoulder. I guess that meant he couldn't tell my knees were shaking every time we had met up. I walked to my car, tucked the cheap burner phone under my tire, and slowly crushed it to smithereens as I drove away.

My next stop after that final meeting with Jim was at the bodega in Margate. I had the big manila bank envelope from my mother's safe deposit box with me in the car. I shoved more bundles of cash from the gym bag into the envelope and then locked my bag in the trunk of my car once I had parked. I made my way inside the bodega. It was weird being in there after all this time. Not much had changed. Bobby was ringing up a few guys at the counter. As they walked out, he came around and gave me a hug. "What brings you to Margate, the cesspool of the north?" he asked. I led him out of the way of the security camera aimed at the counter, and I handed him the envelope. "Bobby, this is for you and Maria. I came into some cash, please don't ask me how, but my mother was looking out for me. I want you guys to have this."

GOOD AT IT

He peeked down into the envelope and looked back up at me. "Carrie. No way. Are you shitting me?" He instinctively dropped his voice. "There's like…a lot of money in here," he looked again, "I mean, Jesus Christ. A lot! No, no, I can't take this," he said, stiffly holding it out to me.

I gently pushed it back towards him. "Please. Don't make a scene. Just take it." He held the envelope. He looked stunned. "Bob, listen," I said, looking around again to be sure no one else was in the store, "There's plenty here for you guys to get out of Margate. Go somewhere else. Anywhere. Start over. Get out of the drug business. You won't need to deal anymore. You and your family can be safe. I want your little girl to have her Dad around for a long time. Quinceanera, graduation, wedding, blah, blah, you know what I mean. She deserves that, and so does Maria. Please. Take it. Go someplace with good schools, nice houses, better neighborhoods. Get a normal job, like at Best Buy or Home Depot or something. Please?" I pleaded with him. "Maybe it sounds selfish, but I want to know you'll be on the other end of the phone every time I call you. That you're not dead over some punks robbing the store or a deal gone sideways. Come on. You know it's only a matter of time. You've always been there for me. Let me do this for you."

"Carrie. I…I don't even know what to say."

"Say you'll do it. Just keep it and say you'll do it."

He looked around the store and took a deep breath, exhaling slowly. He nodded a bit. He watched the two guys standing out front, drinking their cans of beer in paper bags, showing off their tattoos and whistling to some ladies walking by. He rubbed his stubbly face with a heavy sigh.

"You're right," he said, quietly, "We need to get out of here."

"Okay, you know the drill, I'm sure. Only deposit small amounts over time and keep it safe." I said, without holding back a smile.

"Okay, but you gotta know something," he hugged me tightly, "even without this money, I'll always be there for you. I'm always going to be on the other end of the phone."

"I know that, Bobby. But this really locks it in, ya know?"

As he wiped his eyes a bit, he laughed it off, saying "Man, I'd ask if you want to buy some lottery tickets, but ya know…"

"Yeh. I'm good," I said, with a chuckle, as I headed to the door.

"You know I got a cousin down in Marathon. He's a good guy. Fishing buff. Maybe we'll go there. It seems nice."

"Yeah? That's good. I'm thinking about settling down finally in Key West," I said.

"Hey! We'll be close again! How cool is that?"

"Very cool."

"Listen. I'm sorry I didn't keep in touch after we all graduated. That's my bad, ya know? Part of it was that I never wanted you guys around when things got …rough. It was bad enough keeping Maria safe with a kid on the way and all that sort of stuff." His sincerity had such shame. He was looking down at the floor as he explained. I knew what he meant, I could see small scars on his arm, his hand. I knew that things had to have been intense at times.

"Those days are over now. Only good things from now on, yeah?" I tapped the envelope he was holding.

"Yeah," he agreed. He took a deep breath in and slung his big, heavy arm around my shoulder as he walked me to the door.

"Dude, your arm weighs a fucking ton," I say, laughing. He squeezes me harder before letting me go.

GOOD AT IT

"'Cause I'm THE MAN!" he yells out the door after me with a cackle.

Chapter Seven

I felt him watching me as I left. I couldn't look back, or I would have cried, but I was smiling all the way to my car. Knowing Bobby and his family would have a safer life was a huge relief. I knew from an early age that Bobby would fall into some rough business. It was in his nature, given his surroundings. His father was a big, tough Danny Tre'jo looking type. Always had a scowl on his face. He was fierce, always had a baseball bat behind the counter of the store, and god knows what else. His mother was a traditional woman, cooking tamales, paella, and always yelling. Their house was always full of relatives, mostly boys. They were all tattooed, wearing bandanas, plaid shirts with the sleeves ripped off. They were high school dropouts who were constantly looking for a big score, always hustling. So, Bobby's role models couldn't have been worse.

He didn't invite us over often. He said he
didn't want us seeing the mess I always figured
he just didn't want us to hear or see anything bad.
He was street smart and had a heart of gold, and
it felt like he only shared that with us, not "his
boys". He had a softer side. We never felt scared
of anything when Bobby was with us. He was
nurturing and warm but rarely showed that to
anyone but us. I knew having a family of his own
would bring that out more, and I could tell by how
he was with his daughter. He just needed help
getting on track. This was the time. I knew he
wouldn't squander the opportunity. His priority
was his family, and he wanted better for them.
After a few more days of playing it cool, I
convinced Michelle to list her house for sale and
move in with me. One night, while we sat on my
balcony, drinking wine, after carrying the last of
her boxes in, I turned to her.

"Listen, you've been so great about not asking
me anything about the notebook, all that stuff in
the box and my mother's last wishes, but there's
something I need for you to know," I said. "We're
…going to be okay. Better than okay, really. In
her own twisted way, she left me with…a lot," I
paused, "…and she led me back to you, and as

much as I hate to admit it, I think she just may have taught me how to be happy."

"Carrie, I know your relationship with your Mom was strained for the most part, but the one thing I always remember being so in awe of was that, no matter what she had going on, she always wanted you to be happy. I mean, granted, she may not have known how to make that happen, but she never stopped trying. Both Bobby and I used to say to each other 'Just imagine if your Mom actually bothered trying to make you happy instead of just putting food on the table?'...I mean, my parent's focused so hard on the typical things, like proper appearances, good grades, good schools, they hovered all the time and Bobby's parents, well, they just wanted to keep him alive. Like, that was it, that was the goal. Just keeping him alive. But your Mom? She wanted you to be happy. She was always trying. That's something really special."

It got me thinking. When I took an interest in food, she always left me money to get whatever groceries I needed for some weird dish or take me to the market so I could get the things I wanted to experiment with. When I was worried about fitting in at school, she made sure I had the latest sneakers and clothes. It was a lot of little things that I just took for granted but didn't see it as my mother trying to make me happy. At the time, it felt like she was just shutting me up. My mother gave me a lot of freedom as a kid, she wasn't a personal space invader, never rummaged through my room, never questioned my grades or anything. She just trusted I was a good kid. It's weird. Even at times when I didn't trust her, she always trusted me. She was there when I needed her to be. She took shitty situations like my high school suspension and turned it into a teaching moment when she could have just grounded me. She wasn't a normal mother in any way, shape, or form, but she never gave up on trying her best when it came to me. It never occurred to me that my friends saw her any other way than how I did when I was kid, so to hear this from Michelle really made me think about looking at my childhood from a different perspective.

"You're right. It's true. I didn't see it that way when I was younger. But lately, I'm starting to get it. I feel bad that I spent so much time thinking about my relationship with my mother was so awful. Was I a horrible kid?"

"No, oh, baby, no. You were a typical kid. We were all embarrassed or ashamed of our parents at some point or another. The point I was trying to make is that back then the things that bugged you about your Mom were the things Bobby and I envied."

"…and the things that bugged you about your parents were the same things I wished my Mom was doing."

"Yeah and either way, they all did okay. Look at us. We aren't murders or psychos, we don't hurt people, we don't run puppy mills, or take candy from babies,' she laughs as tries to think of other awful offenses.

"We don't toss trash out the car windows, we don't throw rocks at trucks from the overpass," I add.

"Yeah. See? It's all good. Who knows? Maybe your mother's legacy will be that she really did make you happy."

"Well, she did leave us a filthy fucking fortune," I say, shrugging my shoulders. I figured I'd put it that way, without saying how I had to get that filthy fortune.

Michelle smiled and touched my face. "She was always a little unconventional, but she looked out for you in her own way. She kept you out of her tax trouble, she never burdened you with her health issues, she left you money in a safe deposit box, and she was smart enough to know that you loved me, even when you didn't know…so, honey, as long as you're okay with everything, so am I because being with you is all I ever wanted." I nodded and shifted gears before we got too sappy, which isn't our style at all.

"So, listen. I've been looking at a place for us in Key West. I know you love it there. You're going to paint all you want, and I'm going to cook all I want. I don't care if we ever become famous, as long as we're together, doing what we love. How's that sound?"

She leaned over, cupped my face in her hands and kissed me, one of those perfectly soft, long, warm kisses you feel from the inside out. When she slowly backed up, she held my hands and kissed them, before leaning back in her chair.

Michelle had a way of conveying that she knew what the deal was without ever saying it out loud, and that was one of those times. She let out a long, contented sigh and looked around. "Okay. So, I guess we leave all these boxes unpacked for the next move?" I nodded grinning. She leaned back further in her chair and put her feet up on the ledge of the balcony. "Cool."

GOOD AT IT

Within a few months, we were sitting at our perfect little house we bought, located on Casa Marina Court, in Key West, facing the beach that led to the Atlantic Ocean. We loved the big, bright-colored Adirondack chairs on our huge porch. We'd wave to locals riding by on their bicycles and people walking their dogs. We loved that the Key West trolley tour passed by a few times a day. Michelle was always in her paint-smudged overalls, a tank top with a messy ponytail, and she was barefoot just about every day. I loved Key West and always have, but now I could really appreciate it. It was small, eclectic, funky, artsy and full of fun places. After we had settled into the house, we would take daily strolls around the area, sometimes acting like tourists and visiting the Hemingway House, taking catamaran boat trips, snorkelling, getting to know businesses, bars, cafes, taking in some fun drag cabaret shows on balmy evenings at 801 Bourbon Bar, and watching sunsets from Mallory Square. The island of Key West was only four miles long and a mile wide, but it was packed with historical sites, beautiful beaches, and Conch style houses. The port was always filled with cruise ships, the locals were kind and full of knowledge. It felt like the perfect place to settle down.

Bobby and Maria were moving to Marathon Key. Bobby had plans to open his own self-defense and fitness club while Maria stayed home and took care of Carmen. He seemed genuinely happy when we would talk, which was quite often now. We had them over for dinner while they were in town closing on their house. They showed us pictures of their house, and over dessert, Maria shared the news that she was three months pregnant with their second child. "Bobby, I can't believe you kept it a secret!" Michelle said as she punched him in the arm. I hugged Maria. "Carrie, Bobby has something to ask you." I sat back down across from him.

I looked at Bobby, he was just finishing his coffee. He pushed the cup aside and leaned forward a bit. "Look, Care, I can't stop thinking about that day your Mom picked us up from the bus stop and took us out for her Super Fun Day of Fun. I remember wishing my parents were that cool. I mean, yeah, I know she had her shady dealings here and there, and your relationship with her wasn't all roses and peaches, but that day…it was one of the best days ever. What kid wouldn't have loved it? I never want to forget it or… literally any of those times we all spent together. Those were some of the best memories

I have of my youth, ya know? And…now, our lives are different. We're grown-ups. I mean, I never thought we'd own a house or that I'd have a business. A legitimate business. Out of Margate, no less. It's all because of you and your Mom. I don't know a better way to ask but, so I'll just say it: how would you feel about us naming the baby Roseanne if it's a girl?" Maria was standing behind him with her hand on his shoulder. She leaned in, hugging him from behind, resting her face on his shoulder, with a smile. "We'd also like you both to be Godmothers to the baby," she added.

We nodded, like crazy idiots. "Yes, yes, yes!" we both repeated.

Michelle and I were elated. We were, for all intents and purposes, a family. Faults, mistakes, secrets- all those things aside, we had each other's backs and always would. It felt like the worst was behind us, and we were all ready to move forward, breathe easier, and do better.

My mother may have had the right idea all along when it came to money, but I wasn't ready to commit to that idea, because I knew what it would mean about me. I knew what I did. I knew what it made me. It would stay with me forever. I may have a twinge of worry running through me, but let's face, I was used to that. I also knew that my mother must have known I would never continue in her line of work, so this score had to be enough to set me for life. It did. I wasn't going to look back or stay in the game. She knew I wasn't cut out for it on the regular. I'll always wonder if she set it up that way because of who I am, or was it because of who she was. Either way, I'm glad I'm out of the game. I'm pleased it was a one-off. I wanted to lay low, be cool, cook, and live happily. I had grappled with my feelings about my mother my whole life, and one thing was for sure now. I didn't want to look back and be angry with my mother the way I was when I was younger. She was gone now, and I wanted to remember her in a way that would make me smile, not shudder. Not just because of the notebook. Not because of the life I had now. But because she took care of me and now we had a connection.

The thing about my mother is she walked a fine line between being immoral and improper but never crossed it in a way that would ruin us. She kept us intact. She kept us a family at the hardest of times. When I was a whiney little brat who wanted a pool, when I was a snotty, judgemental teenager turning my nose up at her fashion choices, and when I was a secluded, sulky adult out on my own - she never gave up. She had my best interests at heart, even if she made poor choices to keep us afloat and happy. In the end, my mother had my back, and she cared. She was a smart cookie full of sass and flaws, and I was going to try and see things from her point of view and be grateful that she was exactly the way she was. It was better than looking back and being mortified like I had spent half my life already.

I had a gorgeous house now, we upgraded every possible thing in it to make it exactly how we wanted it. I had a fabulous kitchen, I was cooking when I felt like it, taking time to appreciate where I was, what I was looking at, I took comfort in knowing I could literally do anything I wanted to do but didn't have to. I felt relaxed, relieved, and grateful. Michelle and I spent our days happily, lazily, and modestly. Nothing flashy, like my mother always said. Michelle was thrilled to be painting again. Her studio was filling up fast. She loved it. She loved me. She loved painting me. We spent hours talking, walking, laughing, making sandcastles, making love, watching sunsets.

There was something so satisfying about being in love with someone who knows who you, where you came from, shares a lot of the same memories with you and who doesn't try to change you. It's a like being tethered to an anchor, and even if we bounced around a bit at times, we never let go. I always felt safe with Michelle. Even before we were together, just as friends, I felt a safeness with her, and that was a rare feeling for me. From an early age, given my mother's line of work, it became a habit to worry. I was a neurotic kid, and that stuck with me as an adult. Perhaps my mother knew that. Maybe that's why she left me with a perfect plan and a golden future. I didn't have to be neurotic anymore. I had even eased up on my Dad. We were communicating regularly. I sent him a sizeable check, nothing flashy, nothing to raise his suspicion, but enough for some travel so he could come visit us when he had the time. From that point, I'd be able to send him checks more often. It felt good. I didn't elaborate much about the money, I mainly just said I was doing well, and had bought into the restuarnt. He never pressed and was always grateful.

On one gorgeous evening, as we shared a plate of my homemade, pan seared-shrimp with cilantro, lime, and chilies and looked out at the water from our porch as the sun started to set. I was thinking about my Mom, and something dawned on me.

"Can you believe I still don't have a pool?" I asked Michelle jokingly.

"Who needs a pool out back when you have an entire ocean in front of you?"

She breathed in the fresh, salty air, looking at the pink skyline. "Baby, seriously, I don't know what you did to get us here, and I don't want to know, but I can't thank you enough."

We've always just left it as 'my mother left me a lot of money', and that was fine with me because Michelle knows me well enough to know that's not the whole story, but I trust that she will never ask about it. "Cheers, to you... and your mother," She gently clinked my glass of white wine with hers.

"My mother?" I joked, "Oh, please, you never know. I could have robbed the largest jewelry store in Bal Harbour," I said, all smug. She swallowed her wine and slapped my leg with a giggle and squeezed my knee. Smiling, she looked deeply into my eyes, and for a brief second, I wondered if she knew.

Then she burst out laughing, not believing me one bit. "Right. Very funny. Okay. Tell me,

Kermit, was it just like 'The Great Muppet Caper' movie?"

"Exactly like that, Gonzo!" I said, laughing with her.

"Oh, I bet!" she giggled more as she stood up to grab us another bottle of wine in the house.

"And, hey, just so you know, I was good at it!" I called out over my shoulder to her.

"In your dreams!" I could still hear her laughing as I sat there, feeling relaxed. Really, truly relaxed. For the first time in the longest time.

"To you, Mom," I said, raising my glass for a moment, watching the waves roll in and back out.

The End

Made in the USA
Las Vegas, NV
17 December 2020